P9-CFG-427

Cotton in My Sack

Other Books by Lois Lenski

Autobiographical

A LITTLE GIRL OF NINETEEN HUNDRED

Historical

PHEBE FAIRCHILD, HER BOOK
A-GOING TO THE WESTWARD
BOUND GIRL OF COBBLE HILL
OCEAN-BORN MARY
INDIAN CAPTIVE
BLUEBERRY CORNERS
PURITAN ADVENTURE

Regional

BAYOU SUZETTE
STRAWBERRY GIRL
BLUE RIDGE BILLY
JUDY'S JOURNEY
BOOM TOWN BOY
COTTON IN MY SACK
TEXAS TOMBOY
PRAIRIE SCHOOL
MAMA HATTIE'S GIRL
CORN FARM BOY
SAN FRANCISCO BOY
FLOOD FRIDAY
HOUSEBOAT GIRL
COAL CAMP GIRL

Cotton in My Sack

Written and Illustrated by

LOIS LENSKI

J. B. LIPPINCOTT COMPANY

Philadelphia & New York

Chadron State College Library
Chadron, Nebraska

COPYRIGHT, 1949, BY LOIS LENSKI

PRINTED IN THE UNITED STATES OF AMERICA

Eleventh Printing

Library of Congress catalog card number 49-3884

L54c

*For my
beloved
Arkansas
cotton children*

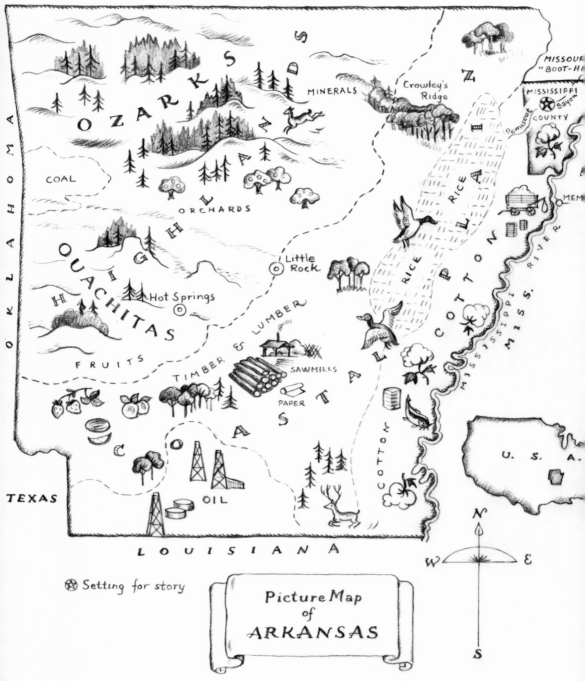

MISSOURI

OZARKS

MINERALS

Crowley's Ridge

MISSOURI "BOOT-HE

MISSISSIPPI

Bayou

PEMISCOT COUNTY

COAL

ORCHARDS

HIGHLAND

OUACHITAS

Little Rock

RICE

RICE

Hot Springs

FRUITS

RICE

PLAIN

COTTON

MEM

MISSISSIPPI RIVER

MISS. RIVER

OKLAHOMA

TIMBER & LUMBER

SAWMILLS

PAPER

COASTAL

COTTON

U. S. A.

TEXAS

OIL

LOUISIANA

⊛ Setting for story

N

W   E

S

Picture Map
of
ARKANSAS

Contents

Foreword

It was Strawberry Girl *who introduced me to my cotton children. They had heard the dramatization over the air and after they had read the book, they wrote to me. They invited me to come to Arkansas and write a book about cotton. I began a delightful correspondence with teachers and children.*

A convenient time came for me to go to Arkansas for a preliminary visit in the spring of 1947. A longer visit was possible in the fall. I was unwilling to write a cotton book without experiencing in every detail all cotton-growing activities.

I entered another world. I donned a sunbonnet, pulled a nine-foot sack and picked cotton with the children. I achieved a sunburned nose, a crick in my back and about half as much cotton as the average ten-year-old picker. Most of my time was not spent picking, however, but studying the actions of the pickers, young and old, making sketches, talking and listening. I observed objectively, yet shared in every happening.

I learned so many things—the weight of a full sack and the weariness it brings; the desirability of a good row and the satisfaction that comes when the bolls are large and the sack fills fast; the length of a day from sunrise—the sun is hot and bright before six in Arkansas—to sunset. I was as eager as anyone to watch the weighing up and see if the desired number of pounds had been accomplished. I climbed on the waiting truck and rode with the town-pickers to their homes in town, while the setting sun flooded the great arch of the sky with red and gold.

FOREWORD

I came to know the cotton children and through stories of personal experiences which they told me, to share their life. As I listened, my admiration and respect for childhood increased, for here at first hand, I saw all its courage, stoicism and fortitude. These children knew what it means to be alive. In their faces I saw a look of that wisdom and kindness which only children know, expressed with ease and certainty.

They had seen sorrow and so they were compassionate. They had seen meanness, and so they valued goodness. They had endured hardship, and so theirs was an attitude not of escape but acceptance. They were ready for whatever life might bring. And because sorrow, meanness and hardship were a part of their lives, they had a better understanding of the joy of living, which comes by a full sharing in human adventure.

Through the children I came to know parents, neighbors and friends. I heard many conflicting points of view on cotton economy, but my primary concern was human character in action, as controlled by an environment. I visited in homes of sharecroppers, tenants and owners alike. I often stayed for meals and felt honored to share a place at the kitchen table. I remember how many questions I asked and how patient everybody was in answering. From my cotton children and their families I learned a great deal more than facts about cotton-growing.

There are more white than Negro sharecroppers in the United States. My cotton family is imaginary, but the incidents used have been taken from real life. Many people, both children and adults, contributed voluntarily, out of their personal experience, to the story.

On Saturdays in town, I sat in a large general store and witnessed a continual moving drama, with Mexicans, Negroes and white people trading, talking and visiting. One day in a thunder storm the electric lights went out and I heard a woman say: "We're all the same color when the lights are out."

An elderly man at a fruit stand, watching it rain, said: "The rain is God's fertilizer. It falls on rich and poor alike."

A colored preacher at a Negro service in a little frame church set in a cotton field said to his congregation: "If you want a friend, first show yourself friendly."

I did not invent these expressions. They came from the people themselves.

It was another and a different world, but I had no feeling of strangeness. I felt as if I had always lived in the cotton country. The cotton people were my people. I was warmed by their kinship and happy in the thought that I belonged.

If this book has anything of their spirit in it, it is because they themselves put it there; and they have, as they well know, my gratitude.

Lois Lenski

Greenacres,
Harwinton, Connecticut
July 1948

The words of the song, "Pick a Bale o' Cotton" are taken from "Git on Board," compiled by Beatrice Landeck, copyright 1944 by Edward B. Marks Music Corporation, New York, and are used by permission. They also appear in "Sing High! Sing Low!" compiled and published by Mary A. Sanders, New York. The words of "Cotton Needs Pickin'" are traditional. A musical arrangement by Clarence Cameron White appears in "Singing America" published by C. C. Birchard & Co., Boston; another arrangement for folk dancing has been published by Charles H. Williams, Hampton Institute, Hampton, Va.

The song Cotton in My Sack *with words written by Lois Lenski and music by Clyde Robert Bulla may be freely used or reprinted by any schools or teachers interested, for the use of their children. Its reprinting for any commercial use is, however, forbidden by copyright. It is hoped that the song will be an incentive to the making of dramatizations of the story.*

Cotton in My Sack

Words by Lois Lenski
Music by Clyde Robert Bulla

STEADILY

SUN UP IN THE MORN-*IN'* HOT UP-ON MY BACK, GOT TO GO START
HOT OLE SUN KEEPS SHIN-*IN'*, HEAV-Y GROWS MY PACK. PICK, PICK, PICK, KEEP

Chorus

PICK-IN' COT-TON IN MY SACK. GOT TO KEEP ON PICK-IN', — GOT TO KEEP ON
PICK-IN' COT-TON IN MY SACK.

PICK-IN', PICK, PICK, PICK, KEEP PICK-IN' COT-TON IN MY SACK. —
SACK, —

— IN MY SACK, — IN MY SACK. —

dim. pp

Cotton in My Sack

CHAPTER I

Home

*"Sun up in the mornin'
Hot upon my back,
Got to go start pickin'
Cotton in my sack . . ."*

Joanda's voice rang out clearly over the cotton field. She
had made up the song herself and its simple tune wavered
uncertainly. Then it stopped.

"Oh!" she cried. "Don't you put that worm on me."

"I will so!" answered Ricky.

She ducked to get out of her brother's way.

"There it is *on* you," said Ricky.

"*Git it off! Git it off!*" screamed Joanda, shaking herself.
"If there's one thing I can't stand about cotton pickin', it's

[1]

worms. Where'd it go? What kind was it—a fuzzy one, or one that's speckeldy-like with lots of feet?"

"I don't know," said Ricky. "You lost it. It's gone now."

"You better git busy and pick," said Joanda.

Five-year-old Ricky sat down in the cotton row. "I *can't* pick and I *won't* pick," he said.

"When you take a notion to pick, you *can* pick," said Joanda.

"What we got to pick for?" asked Ricky.

"This is Daddy's cotton," explained Joanda. "We're pickin' for Big Charley, Daddy's boss-man."

"Is Daddy gonna pay me?" asked Ricky.

"Daddy's *s'posed* to pay *me* for pickin', but sometimes he don't," said Joanda.

"When I git my money, I'm gonna git me a new coat," said Ricky.

"You'll be an old man before you git it," said Joanda.

Ricky slung his tow sack over his shoulder and began to pick. "I'm gonna git my sack full."

Joanda started a game she had made up: "Do you chew tobacco?"

"No," said Ricky, shaking his head.

"Do you dip snuff?"

"NO!" answered Ricky.

"Do you smoke a pipe?"

"NO, NO, NO!" shouted Ricky.

"Do you eat popcorn?"

"No—oh yes! YES!"

"Do you chew gum?"

[2]

"YES MA'M, when I can git it!" laughed Ricky.

The small boy held out both hands filled with cotton. "Look how much cotton I got!" He had a sweet smile. His face was plump, but it was very dirty. "For Christmas I want a tractor. I'm gonna be a farmer."

"It's a long time 'fore Christmas comes," said his sister. She stopped in her row and lifted the middle of her seven-foot pick sack to shake the cotton down to the end. Her face was pretty, but had a wistful, sad expression. Dark brown eyes looked out from under her floppy checked sunbonnet. Tangled brown hair hung beside her cheeks. She wore baggy patched blue jeans and a faded red plaid shirt.

"After it's shook down it's not half full," she said. "If I could only git it full once, I'd be happy. Daddy says I won't be even half-a-hand till I git it full."

"Am I a full hand?" asked Ricky.

Joanda laughed. "You? Course not. Mavis is fourteen— she's a full hand, only she can't pick now 'cause she's got a boil on her neck. Steve's twelve, but he's not half-a-hand 'cause he stands and looks around so much. You have to be eleven or twelve to be a full hand."

"Oh!" said Ricky.

"Bless Pat!" cried Joanda suddenly. "That's our baby crying."

"Maybe it's Mr. Burgess's cotton pickers singin'," said Ricky. "I hear our dog barking. *Here, Trouble, here, Trouble!*" He called, but the dog did not come.

The children looked down to the far end of the rows, where three bent figures were picking.

[3]

"Listen how the baby's hollerin'," Joanda went on. "Bet she's cryin' to come over here to me. Bet she'd be quiet if she was here with me. Mama won't git her sack full if Lolly keeps on yellin'."

"I'm gonna pull my shoes off," announced Ricky.

"Mama'll whoop you. Daddy'll whoop you," said Joanda.

"No, they won't," answered Ricky.

"Big Charley, the boss-man will whoop you."

"No, he won't!"

"Miz Shands will whoop you."

"She jest better not try it," laughed Ricky. "She'd have to ketch me first."

"You'll git sandburrs in your feet," warned Joanda.

Ricky walked around in the dirt. "I ain't got no cuckle-burrs," he said.

"Pick some more, sugar," said Joanda. "Pick four more pounds, then you can rest."

"I'm tard of pickin'," said Ricky. "I ain't never gonna pick no more cotton as long as I live."

Joanda laughed. The children had picked to the end of their row and now came out on the turn-row between two cotton fields. Here stood the trailer, three-quarters full of cotton. It was an old rickety cotton wagon, with high board sides. Ricky started to climb up the ladder at the back.

"Daddy don't want you to git on the cotton," warned Joanda. "Git down, Ricky." He kept on climbing.

"Cotton feels good on my bare feet, so soft and squnchy," said the boy. He jumped and came down *plop*. He rolled over and over, the fuzzy cotton sticking to his clothes. "I like to go barefooted. It feels good on my toes!"

"We don't have to go barefooted now," said Joanda. "We got shoes to wear. We used to go barefooted when we didn't have money to buy any."

"My shoes hurt my feet," said Ricky. "One time I had some money and I spent it."

"I got $3.45 now, I had $5.00," said Joanda proudly. "I spent it for groceries. I got baloney and bread and two cans of fish and two candy bars. Steve owes me a quarter. He better pick cotton and pay it back. If he don't, I'll make him. He says he's goin' to, but if he don't, I'll take my switch after him."

The Negro pickers in the next field were singing. Joanda stood still to listen:

> " 'Oh, the cotton needs pickin' so bad!
> Cotton needs pickin' so bad,
> Cotton needs pickin' so bad,
> Gonna pick all over dis field" . . .

"Mama and Daddy's pickin' fast," said Ricky. The children looked at the three figures who were coming closer and closer.

"Why is Steve so far behind the others?" asked Ricky.

"He's lookin' at every bird and wishin' it was an airplane," said Joanda. "He's lookin' at the cars along the road." She pointed to the highway off on the right.

"Where's all the cars a-goin'?" asked Ricky.

"To town," said Joanda.

"I don't want to live in town," said Ricky. "You can't make any money in town."

[5]

("I do," said Joanda. "You can spend all your money in town.) Let's ask Daddy to go to the gin this evenin', when he takes the cotton in."

"Goody, goody!" cried Ricky, jumping up and down.

All the time she had been talking, the girl's nimble fingers had been putting cotton in her sack, as she started on the next row. Her bent back moved from plant to plant, and her thin arms moved in a steady rhythm.

"Why don't you rest a while?" asked Ricky.

"I don't rest, I have to keep on workin'," said Joanda. "I picked twenty-seven pounds one evenin'. Maybe if I try hard, I'll git my pick sack *full*."

"*Here, Trouble, here, Trouble!*" called Ricky.

A little gray dog came tearing down the cotton middle, barking. Then Daddy came, carrying his bulging sack over his

shoulder. He was a thin man with a weathered face, and he wore a slouchy felt hat. Mama came more slowly, dragging her heavy load. Joanda ran to meet her. Mama's load was not all cotton, for there on her pick sack rode the baby, Lolly, as comfortable as a bird in a nest.

"Lolly rolled off back down there," said Mama, "and how she did yell. When I looked around, there was Trouble sittin' in her place as smart as you please, expectin' a ride."

"Betcha he pushed her off," said Joanda. "Can I take her, Mama?"

"Land sakes, yes, git her off," said Mama. "My back's nigh broke. She's as heavy as a ton o' bricks."

"Betcha she was hollerin' for me," said the girl. "Betcha she missed me all right."

Mama had so many clothes on, it was hard to tell whether she was a large or small woman. She wore pants to cover her legs, her cotton dress came to her knees, and over it she wore one of Daddy's old shirts to cover her arms. Brown eyes peered out from under her large slat bonnet. Hot, tired and dirty, she slipped down on her cotton sack to rest.

Joanda took Lolly on her lap, her thin arms squeezed tightly around the heavy two-year-old. The baby was plump and had curly red hair. She was dressed in a khaki coverall suit with red buttons down the front. Joanda looked down at her, adoration in her eyes.

"Lolly pick cotton? Lolly like to pick cotton?" she asked.

Lolly reached over and pulled off a fluffy boll. She began to make a humming sound.

"You singin', Lolly? You singin' *Cotton in my Sack?*"

[7]

Joanda turned to Mama. "Lolly makes out like she's singin', Mama."

"Only time that young un's quiet is when she's eatin' or sleepin'," said Mama. "She's the noisiest little somebody."

Joanda gave the baby a tight hug.

Daddy began weighing. He tied the two ends of his long pick sack together and hooked them over the scales. "Fifty-two pounds," he said. "Git off that sack, you two."

Mama and Joanda stood up and watched as he weighed the others. Mama had forty-four pounds, Joanda eighteen and Ricky seven. Daddy marked all the weights down in a little green record book. Steve came up, and he had thirty pounds. Daddy shook his head. "We'd a had more if Mavis coulda picked today. Cotton's light. It don't weigh much when it's plumb dry."

Each sack, after being weighed, was thrown up on top of the load. Mama took the baby and Joanda climbed up to help. Ricky and Joanda and Steve and Daddy jumped up and down, emptying the sacks and tramping the cotton. Trouble jumped and bounced and barked.

Mama looked down at Lolly and said, "They're havin' a time, ain't they?" Lolly clapped her hands and laughed.

"Can we go to the gin?" "Oh, Daddy, can we?" "Mama, can we ride to the gin?" begged the children.

Mama looked at Daddy who nodded his head.

"I reckon so," answered Mama. "Come, Trouble. We'll go see if Mavis has got supper cooked." She started across the field, baby in arms and dog at her heels.

Daddy's truck, already full of cotton, had been left parked

in the turn-row. He backed it up, hitched the trailer on, and drove out of the cotton field. Joanda threw off her sunbonnet to cool her face in the breeze. The children sat down on the cotton. Their bright faces and figures, seated on the white cotton, made a colorful pattern against the blue of the sky. A radiant sunset threw out flames of red and gold, casting changing shadows across the level Arkansas fields. The truck bumped along the dirt road until it came to the crossroads center, where beside a garage and a country store, stood the White Top cotton gin.

Daddy drove up under the shed until the trailer was on the scales.

A man hurried out. "Hi there, Dave Hutley!"

The children hopped down and the man weighed the cotton. He went in the building to mark down the weight, came out and hooked a tag on the trailer. Then Daddy backed up and he weighed the cotton in the truck.

"O. K., Hutley," the man called out.

Daddy drove the trailer under a large round pipe which came down from the main part of the gin. The man jumped on the load and began to move the pipe about. A loud noise was heard as the motor was turned on and the fan began to operate. The suction pulled the cotton up into the pipe.

"That's the suck!" Joanda explained to Ricky. "See how it sucks up all the cotton?" She turned to Steve. "What do they do with the cotton after they git it in the gin?"

"Don't *you* know?" answered Steve. "They've got big machinery in there. It separates the seeds from the cotton and blows the hulls out in a big pile at the back. The seeds go out in another place. And the cotton goes round and round till it gits clean of leaves and trash, then it's pressed in a bale."

"They put a tow sack around it and tie it with wires," said Joanda. "I know that much."

"Big Charley, our boss-man, took me in and showed me all over one time," said Steve.

"Oh look, what's that up there in our cotton?" cried Joanda. "It's something blue . . . it's . . . whish! There, it's gone. *It was my sunbonnet!*"

"It went so quick!" cried Ricky, laughing. "I saw it go."

"You left it on the cotton," said Steve. "Wasn't it funny to see it go up?"

Joanda didn't know whether to laugh or cry. She started for the door of the gin.

"Where you a-goin'?" called Steve. "Kids are not allowed in there."

"Gonna git my sunbonnet," said Joanda, "before anything happens to it."

Daddy came up and the children explained.

"You're too late, sugar," said Daddy. "It's all chawed up to bits by this time."

"Chawed up?" Joanda blinked. She was used to sudden losses and things she could not help.

After the cotton was unloaded, the man said, "Goin' home now? You live in that shotgun house out on the by-o road, don't you?"

The children climbed into the cab of the truck with Daddy. As they rode along the dusty dirt road, Ricky asked, "Daddy, what's a shotgun house?"

Daddy laughed. "Where'd you hear that, son?"

"The man at the gin said we lived in one," answered Ricky.

"That's right," said Daddy. Now they were close enough to see the house, which was painted red. "It has three rooms in a row. I can take my shotgun and shoot through the front door and the bullet will go out the back door. It will go plumb through all four doors in a straight line."

The children laughed.

"But you won't do it, will you, Daddy?" asked Ricky.

"I got better use for my gun than any sech fool doin's," said Daddy. "Might better go squirrel huntin' over in them woods along the Mississippi River, eh, boys?"

"You bet!" agreed Steve.

The small yard around the house was bare of grass and untidy with trash. Near the back door was a pile of coal and beyond were several rickety sheds. Cotton grew close on all sides. There was just room for Daddy to park the truck and trailer close to the front porch.

The children ran around and went in at the back door. Mama was bent over the stove, putting coal in. Hot bacon fat sizzled angrily and sent up an appetizing odor. A few dishes were set on the oilcloth table.

"I lost my sunbonnet, Mama," said Joanda. "I left it on top of the cotton. It went up in the suck and got chawed to bits."

"Why didn't you keep it on your head where it belongs?" said Mama. "You'll have to find another old one to wear. Mavis didn't even git the fire started. She's still in bed in there. And Lolly's been cryin' so . . . Take her, Nannie."

Joanda picked up the baby and went through to the front part of the house. Mavis lay on one of the two double beds that nearly filled the middle room. Joanda was hot and tired after her all-day picking. A gentle breeze came in at the open front door. Joanda sat on the floor and played with the baby. Then Lolly crawled off to explore. Joanda stretched out full length.

Her tired back felt better when she lay flat on the floor. She rested, not moving, her head placed near the wall. Then she looked up. There on the wall old newspapers were pasted, in place of plaster. They were stained and dirty, but she could still read the words and study the pictures and advertisements. The papers were pasted on upside-down. She could read them better lying on the floor.

Joanda loved to read. There were no books or magazines in the house, only the newspapers on the wall. The words—strange words she did not know the meaning of—had a fascination for her. She used to ask Daddy to explain what they meant. But he couldn't—he only went to the third grade, he said. Joanda could pronounce them, if she took one syllable at a time and tried to say them slowly.

" 'Perm—a—nent, permanent—lasts forever.' They do something to the hair, I reckon. $5.00—that's too much," Joanda said to herself. "But it sure does look purty." She must save up all the hard words she did not know and ask the teacher when she went back to school.

"Supper's ready!" called Mama from the kitchen.

Mama knew how to cook supper, but she did not know the magic of words.

CHAPTER II

Saturday in Town

O*h, it's Saturday—beautiful Saturday!* The minute she woke up, Joanda felt happy all over. Saturday was the most wonderful day of the week because the whole family went to town. Town was a magic place on Saturday, because all the people had money to spend.

After Daddy's cotton was picked, the Hutleys had started picking for J. T. Burgess, and were paid off in cash every night. On Saturday, they went to town to spend the money.

Right after breakfast they climbed into the truck. Mama and Daddy took Lolly in the cab with them. The other four children stood up in the back. It was a five-mile ride to town. The sun was already hot and the wind blew their hair in the breeze. They rode along the dirt road to the crossroad, then took the smooth highway.

When they got to town it was like a parade, so many cars and trucks going down Main Street. Cars in front and in back of them. Cars parked on both sides. The children leaned over the high board sides of the truck. They could see everything —the cars, the people, the stores. But the crowds on the side-walks did not notice them at all.

Daddy always parked in the same place, in an empty lot back of the Beehive store. They got out and Daddy gave Mama a ten-dollar bill. The children had the money they had earned for picking cotton. Ricky had a dollar, Joanda had her $3.45 and the older children had more because they were faster pickers. Mavis and Joanda had their money in bright red purses they had bought the week before. The boys carried theirs in their pockets.

The Hutleys did what they always did. First they walked down the street and just looked. There was so much to see. All the show-windows were full of tempting things to buy, and many stores had things set out on the sidewalks.

So often when they came to town, they had no money in their pockets at all. Now, in cotton-picking time, it was differ-ent. They had money and anything could happen. All the things they saw took on a shining glory because they were within their reach—rings, gold watches, bracelets, jewelry, anything. Joanda walked on wings, looking hard. *I can have that, I can have that*, she kept saying to herself. *I can have all these things if I want them.* She had never known happiness like this.

They paused in front of Atkins' furniture store.

"I'd like a couch like that," said Mama softly. "If I paid

[17]

something down on it, it wouldn't take but about three or four months, I don't guess."

But she did not go in. The most fun was thinking what you *might* buy, even if you didn't.

The Hutleys saw the one-armed hot tamale man. He had a high yellow box, with the words HOT TAMALES on it, set on a three-wheeled cart. The cart held a fire to keep the tamales hot. The tamales were made of groundup peppered pork and cornmeal. They had been wrapped in cornshucks and steamed.

"Want a tamale?" asked Daddy.

"No, they're too hot," said Ricky. "I had one once and it burned my tongue."

The Hutleys walked on. Suddenly they heard music and Lolly began to clap her hands. They stopped and listened. A man and a woman came shuffling along sideways in front of Carter's drug store. The man had a guitar strapped across his shoulder, with a tin cup on the end. He began to strum the guitar and to sing in a hollow voice:

> *"Now we are aged and gray, Maggie,*
> *The trials of life are nearly done . . ."*

"The man's blind," whispered Mama.

"But the woman can see," said Joanda. "She leads him and takes care of him."

"Pretty bad shape they're in," said Mama, shaking her head.

"Always somebody worse off than we are," said Daddy.

"*We* got money!" whispered Ricky.

Mama looked at Daddy and then they all put some money

in the man's cup. Joanda gave one of her dimes.

"God bless you," said the blind man.

The Hutleys came to the Star Movie Theater, but it had not opened yet. The picture was called *Six Shootin' Sheriff*. They studied the scenes in the glass cases.

"I'm comin' back and see this," said Steve.

"So'm I," said Mavis. "It's got outlaws in it."

A man had a popcorn stand at the theater entrance. The popping corn sent out an inviting fragrance. Daddy said, "Let's have some popcorn." So he bought seven sacks, one for each, and they stood and ate it.

Lolly squatted on the sidewalk and dipped her fat hands into her sack. Ricky perched on a sack of potatoes in front of the grocery next door to eat his. Steve and Mavis took theirs and walked on. Ricky ate his up first and Daddy bought him a second sack. When that was gone, Daddy gave him half of his.

"How long can you keep this up, Ricky?" he asked.

"Till I starve to death!" answered the boy.

Daddy and Mama laughed. Suddenly Lolly began to sputter.

"Take that popcorn away from the baby before she chokes," said Mama.

Joanda took Lolly's sack away and gave her Ricky's empty one. Lolly threw it down and began to howl. She snatched her own bag from Ricky, dropped it and scattered the popcorn all over the sidewalk. A fresh wind blew it in all directions. Lolly ran to chase the rolling kernels.

"Don't let her eat 'em, they're nasty," said Mama.

Joanda picked Lolly up. They walked on down the street.

[19]

"You're fixin' to git some new duds, ain't you, Neva?" asked Daddy.

"Sure thing," said Mama.

They went to the Beehive for clothes. Dresses and suits hung across in front of the store, flapping in the wind. A table of True Blue shoes stood outside. People could choose what they wanted before they went in. Mavis and Steve were waiting at the entrance.

"I ain't seen a soul I know," complained Mavis. She had a towel bandage round her neck which made her hold her head to one side. "Nobody's in town but us."

"You'll see everybody in Mississippi County, Arkansas, before the day's over," laughed Daddy. "Well, I reckon I'll just mosey along."

"Dave," said Mama, "you won't . . ."

"Don't you worry, Neva," said Daddy.

"We'll wait for you at the Goodwill," said Mama, "when we git through our tradin'." As Daddy walked away, Mama looked after him anxiously.

Ricky pulled on Mama's sleeve. "Buy me a buggy bicycle, Mama."

"I just bought you one two weeks ago," said Mama.

"Joanda won't let me ride on it," said Ricky. "She's mean."

"Yes she will," said Mama. "It's too little for her."

"Buy me a tractor then . . ."

They went into the Beehive and they all got new clothes, the girls each a cotton dress and sweater, the boys overalls, shirts and caps. When they came out they had bulky packages under their arms. They stopped at Hank's hot-dog stand and bought hot-dogs and cold drinks.

They came to the Goodwill, a big brick store that covered half a block. It said GOODWILL FOR EVERYBODY across the top. Here, everything was sold—groceries, dry goods, notions, hardware, seeds and farm machinery. It was a common meeting place for the country people. A radio on a chair outside the store door blared hillbilly music. Mama and the children stopped to listen.

Then they went in. Mama looked around and saw the Suttons, Jed and Maggie, at the blanket counter. It had a sign that said: *Use our Lay Away Plan 50¢ Down on Any Blanket.* Maggie carried a stove pipe with an elbow, and Jed had a coal bucket hanging on his arm.

"Buyin' you some blankets?" asked Mama.

"Yes *ma'm*," said Jed, "gittin' ready for winter."

Mama laughed. "Oh, winter's a long time off. How's your cotton?"

"As sorry a crop as I ever saw in my life," said Maggie. "I'm sick and sore all over, couldn't sleep but two hours last night. My fingers are plumb stiff from pickin' cotton, but I can't sit still in the house till it's done picked. We lack three bales of gittin' ours out."

"We got part of ours out," said Mama. "We been pickin' for J. T. while we're waitin' for the rest of ours to open up."

Maggie began to talk about her ills. "I told the Lord if He'd save me, I'd never fool with doctors no more."

Mama sighed sympathetically. "I wisht I had faith like that . . ."

Just then the Burgesses, who were the Hutley's nearest neighbors, came up. There were J. T. and Mrs., who was always called "Aunt Lessie," and all four children. The boys, Bug and T. W., nicknamed Tightwad, took Steve off between them to go to the moving-picture show. Mavis went away with the twins, Arlene and Jolene. J. T. talked awhile, then went off with Jed Sutton. That left the women alone with the younger children.

"Got through your tradin'?" asked Mrs. Burgess.

"Law, no, I ain't begun," said Mama, "but my money's gone."

Joanda held Lolly up and Mrs. Burgess said: "Ain't she a sight!"

"She's proud to see you, Aunt Lessie," said Joanda.

"Sech curls. She sure favors you, Neva," said Mrs. Burgess.

"Face dirty and the day just half over," laughed Mama.

"Some folks' cotton ain't but six inches tall," began Mrs. Sutton. "It's the least I ever seen. Last year it was high as my head—I could hide myself in it."

"Not enough rain this summer," said Mama.

"In summer when we need it, it don't rain," said Mrs. Burgess. "In fall, time to pick cotton, it goes to rain."

The store was filled with family groups, some buying, others

visiting. Mexicans and Negroes city and country people filled
the aisles. Joanda put Lolly down on the floor. The baby began to run around the store, between and under the counters,
bumping into strangers, tumbling down and getting up again.
Joanda followed, laughing.

Ricky came up, his mouth full of candy. Lolly snatched a
lollipop out of his hand and ran off with it. Ricky chased, but
could not catch her. She went running out the street door.

Suddenly, fear clutched at Joanda's heart. Lolly was running into danger. The streets and sidewalks were more
crowded than ever. Joanda hurried out to find her. Beside the
door stood a man, with a box on his left arm, selling shoestrings
and chewing gum.

"Did you see a little girl with red hair come out the door
jest now?" asked Joanda.

The man pointed: "Way down yonder she goes like a streak of lightnin'."

Joanda dashed through the crowd and found her little sister almost at the curb. She picked her up and brought her back to the store. She saw Ricky beside the candy counter, sucking a lollipop. "How many lollipops you had?" she asked.

"Six," said Ricky. "Jest gonna git me some more."

He paid his money, took the candy and went over to the toy counter. There he bought a balloon and began to blow it up. It was a long, thin one with a snake head on the end. He blew it at his sister.

"You jest better not blow that horrid thing at me," said Joanda, "or I'll bust it." Anger flitted across her thin face. "You know I hate snakes."

Ricky kept on shoving the balloon closer and closer. Joanda put the baby down and snatched at the balloon. Ricky dodged and jerked away. The balloon suddenly popped like a pistol and fell to the floor in bits.

Everybody turned to look. Joanda and Ricky smiled at each other, but Lolly began to cry. The clerk said, "She's cryin' for a purty."

"I'll git you a play-purty, Lolly," said Joanda, "if you'll hush up. What you want—a bunny or a dolly? A colorin' book? Peanuts?"

Lolly pointed to everything she saw. Sometimes Joanda said, "No, you can't have that," but more often she made the purchase. Soon Joanda's arms were filled with packages.

"You buyin' her all them things?" asked Ricky.

"She has to have somethin'," said Joanda. "Nobody else

buys her a thing. Each thing I show her, she cries for it. I tell her she's not gonna git it, but she *makes* me buy it. I spend more on her than on me."

"Lolly can't color no colorin' book," said Ricky. "She can't even hold a pencil."

"I can color it for her, can't I?" said Joanda hotly.

"Oh, you jest want it for yourself!" said Ricky. "Why don't you buy one for *me?*"

"Go buy a little ole coloring book for yourself if you want one!" snapped Joanda. "If you ain't spent all your money on stuff to eat and I s'pose you have!"

She looked around and saw Lolly running away again. *"She's takin' off!"* Joanda rushed to her mother, dumped her packages and ran out. *"Which way? Which way did she go?"*

But the shoestring man hadn't seen her and didn't know which way she went. Joanda looked at the cars and trucks and shuddered. What if Lolly got run over? She would die if anything happened to Lolly, she loved her so much.

Ever since Lolly was born, Joanda had taken care of her. Always, Joanda was the one who could quiet her. Joanda knew that Lolly liked her better than anybody in the family. *She's crazy about me, because I like her so much. She won't let me git three inches away from her. Every time she cries the least bit I pick her up. . . .*

And now Lolly was gone and it was all Joanda's fault. She should have kept tight hold of her hand. Lolly was only two, though most people took her for three. She was still a baby who needed looking after. Joanda ran so hard she didn't look where she was going. Before she knew it, she bumped headlong into some one coming the other way. *Oh dear, it's one of them stuck-up people—a woman with a hat on*, she thought. She drew back quickly.

"Little girl, why don't you look where you are going, if you're in such a hurry?" said the woman sharply. Then she saw who is was. "Why, Joanda, it's *you*. I'm surprised."

Joanda recognized her. It was Mrs. Shands, the wife of Big Charley, Daddy's boss-man.

"*Yes ma'm,*" she gasped. "I . . . er . . . Lolly . . ." but she could not take time to explain, so on she went.

Breathless, Joanda searched. She ran up and down the block, she crossed the street and went up and down the other side. She came back and went round the entire block. She went in the Goodwill store, looked under the counters and through the aisles. She asked Mama and Mrs. Burgess, who

were standing at the lunch counter, drinking coffee. Mama said, "Go find her." Joanda asked strange people, but no one knew or cared. *I'll have to ask a cop soon . . . that's the cop out in the middle of the street. I know, 'cause cops have guns,* and she was terrified at the thought. She knew she could never get up that much courage, even to save her beloved Lolly.

She stopped suddenly. She was trembling all over and breathing hard. The tears came in a flood, she could not hold them back. She buried her face in her hands.

"That you, Nannie?" She heard a man's voice. "What's the matter?"

Joanda looked up. It was J. T. Burgess and he was smiling as if nothing could possibly be wrong.

"Lolly's lost! Lolly's lost and I don't know which way to go!" cried Joanda. "She let go my hand and took off . . ."

"She's not at the Goodwill?" asked J. T. quietly.

"I went back and looked," said Joanda. "Mama and Aunt Lessie said she wasn't there. They told me to go hunt."

"There's only one other place she knows to go. Let's have a look."

J. T. led Joanda to the Beehive and down the alley at the side. They went to Daddy's truck, and there in the bed, on a pile of tow sacks lay Lolly, sound asleep.

"She came to a safe place—the little tyke," said J. T., laughing. "I told you we'd find her. Now, see you don't lose her again."

Lolly woke up and Joanda took her in her arms. She held her tightly as if she would never let her go again. With a thankful heart, she carried her back to the store. Mrs. Burgess had gone away and Mama was still waiting for Daddy to come. Mama had been standing all this time. There were no chairs at the store.

Lolly grew sleepy again and too heavy to hold. Joanda sat down on one of the lower shelves of the men's coat counter. She made a bed for the baby on the pile of coats and leaned against them to rest. Ricky curled up beside her and fell asleep with his head in her lap. After a while, Mavis and Steve came back, full of excitement over the show.

"*Six Shootin' Sheriff* was wonderful," said Mavis. "At first I couldn't tell who was the outlaw and who was goin' to ketch who . . ."

"It was clear as daylight," said Steve. "They had a bunch of cattlemen and some wicked guys that did some rustlin'. I knew jest what was goin' to happen and it did."

"Got any money left?" asked Mama in a dull voice.

"No," said Mavis and Steve.

"Did you buy anything to take home?" asked Mama.

"No," they said. "You kept our clothes packages, didn't you?"

"Yes," said Mama. "You had anything to eat?"

"Hot-dogs and ice cream and cold drinks . . . and candy and . . ."

"You seen Daddy anywhere?"

"No," they said.

"I don't know where all the money went," said Mama sadly. "We had plenty when we started out. We shoulda bought our winter groceries first thing. I wanted Daddy to git some last week, but he didn't and now . . ."

[29]

The crowd in the store had thinned out. It was supper time, but the store would be open until nine. Suddenly darkness fell and with the going of the sun, the glamour of the bright day faded.

"Let's go to the truck and wait for Daddy," said Mama. "We can't buy no supper because we've spent all our money. If Daddy has any left . . ." but she knew he wouldn't.

Mama carried Lolly to the truck. The three little ones curled up on the front seat, leaned against Mama and fell asleep. Mavis and Steve sat on the back and dangled their legs over. They talked on and on about the show.

After a long time, men's voices were heard and Joanda woke up. She looked out the cab window and saw two men helping a limp figure along. She heard J. T.'s voice and it comforted her.

"Here's Dave, Neva," said J. T. "He couldn't make it himself, so we brought him. Got some sacks in the truck?"

"Yes," said Mama. The men helped Daddy in.

"I'll drive you folks home," said J. T. "Lessie took our kids home a good while ago."

"I sure do thank you," said Mama. The truck started with a clatter.

Beautiful Saturday . . . all its magic was gone, but Joanda was too tired to notice. She dozed off to sleep again.

CHAPTER III

School

"Can I wear my new red dress, Mama?" called Joanda.
"That's what I got it for," answered Mama.

"And Ricky his new overalls and shirt?"

"Yes," said Mama. "I want him to look nice on his first day at school."

"I'll git his ears clean," said Joanda.

They were washing at the shelf on the back porch. Joanda put the washrag into the basin and rubbed it hard with soap. Then she dug into the boy's ears.

"Stop hurtin' me! Stop hurtin' me!" screamed Ricky.

It was late November and the "cotton vacation" was over. The rural school at Delta Flats had opened a few days before. It was called a "split-term school" since it was closed during the cotton-picking season, September, October and part of November, because all the children picked cotton. The time lost was made up by a six weeks' summer session in July and August.

"I hear the Burgess kids comin'," said Mama. They lived a quarter mile up the road on the other side.

Mavis and Steve hurried out to join the Burgess boys and the twins. Swinging their lunches, the children walked off down the dirt road. Joanda and Ricky hurried to catch up.

Joanda's new dress was red with white polka dots. Her new sweater was red too, so she felt very proud. As she walked along, she kept putting her hands in the two pockets of the dress. She had never had pockets before.

Ricky looked fine in his new clothes, but Joanda could see he was scared. She tried her game *Do you chew tobacco?* on him, but he would not play. He dipped his hand in his paper lunch sack, brought out a biscuit spread with molasses and began to eat. Joanda didn't tell him not to. She knew just how he felt.

She was a little scared herself, because she knew there would be a strange teacher. It might be a better one than they had in the summer term, or it might be a worse one. But Joanda had been in two different schools before, so she felt much more experienced than Ricky.

"*Nannie, Nannie!*" called a shrill little voice behind her.

Joanda stopped. There was Lolly coming as fast as her two fat legs could carry her.

"Oh dear!" sighed Joanda. "Now I'll be late. I gotta take her all the way back."

She picked up her baby sister and ran back to the house.

She put her on one of the beds, closed the door and called to Mama: "Watch Lolly. Don't turn her loose!"

She flew down the road again and caught up to Ricky. His lunch was gone now. He threw the sack in the ditch. Still Joanda didn't say anything. He seemed to be always hungry. She decided to give him half of her lunch at dinnertime.

The sun was so warm and bright they hardly needed their sweaters. By noon it would be hot. The dirt road was filled with dry, uneven ruts. There were cotton fields on both sides, with stalks drying up and losing their fresh green. There were no fences. Across the landscape, small sharecropper houses could be seen set in rows along other dirt roads. A fringe of trees followed Pemiscot Bayou a quarter of a mile to the right. Soon the children came to the little crossroads center. The schoolhouse was just beyond the country store.

All the children were playing in the yard when they came up. They were choosing up sides for *Sugarloaf Town*. The school looked different. The old iron pump was gone, and a new room had been added to the two-room frame building.

Jolene Burgess explained: "It's a kitchen. They're gonna serve a hot dinner every day. They cook it on a stove."

"We brought our dinner from home," said Joanda.

"So did we," whispered Jolene. "We're not gonna eat the stuff they cook."

"Teacher won't let you eat your cold lunch," said Shirley Mason, a fourth grade girl. "There's two new teachers and they're gonna make everybody eat what they cook."

"Mama knew all about it," said Joanda. "Miz Burgess told

[33]

her. We didn't bring money to pay for a hot dinner. Mama wants us to eat our own stuff."

Joanda took Ricky by the hand and clutched her lunch sack more tightly. She made up her mind she would not be scared, no matter what happened.

The bell rang and they all crowded in at the door. Steve and Mavis went with the older children into the upper grade room, Joanda and Ricky into the lower. Joanda was in Fourth and Ricky in First. Their new teacher's name was Miss Fenton. She was a large woman with dark hair and eyes. She had a friendly smile.

The Readers were the same as in the summer and Joanda was glad to see hers again. She could read it all the way through. It was easy. While the little children were having a lesson, Miss Fenton asked the larger ones to write a story. It was to be something they knew about.

Joanda thought and thought, but couldn't think of anything. Then she looked down in her lap and saw her red dress. That gave her an idea. So she wrote:

"The Red Dress"

"I have a new dress. My Mama bought it at the Beehive Store. It has deep pockets. Today I wanted to wear the red dress with deep pockets. My Mama let me wear it today. I wish I could wear the red dress every day. The red dress is very pretty. I never had pockets before. I am glad I wore it today."

Miss Fenton liked Joanda's story and had her read it aloud.

[34]

Joanda hung her head and felt very shy when the teacher said how good it was.

Before she knew it, it was noontime. Miss Fenton told all the children about the hot lunch and told them to tell their parents. Those who could pay fifteen cents a day should bring the money, but those who could not pay would have a free lunch. It would be fun to all eat together in the new dining room. Most of the children got up and went out.

Joanda took Ricky by the hand and went to the table in the corner where she had left her lunch sack.

"We brought our dinner from home," she told the new teacher.

"All right," said Miss Fenton, "but try and bring the money tomorrow."

"Mama won't let us," said Joanda. "She wants us to eat our own stuff."

Miss Fenton said nothing but left the room. The cold lunch children sat around the table and began to eat. Soon Miss Fenton came back with glasses and a pitcher of milk. Joanda and Ricky shook their heads.

"Do you get milk at home?" asked Miss Fenton.

"Yes ma'm," said Joanda.

"You have a cow then?"

"No ma'm," said Joanda. "It's Carnation milk. We git it out of a can. Lolly's the fattest baby Mama ever had. That's 'cause she drinks it."

Miss Fenton smiled and filled their glasses.

Joanda divided her biscuits and cold boiled sweet potatoes with Ricky. They ate fast but did not touch the milk. Like the other children, Joanda threw her paper sack in the waste basket.

Out in the hall, everybody was looking at the bubble fountain. An electric pump had been installed and water piped into the building. The water bubbled up in a little fountain and the children leaned over and drank. Joanda and Ricky watched. Then Bug Burgess put his fingers on the spout and sprinkled water over the crowd. They all ran.

The afternoon passed quickly and happily. Ricky was so good in school, Joanda was pleased. He sat very still and listened. He did just what the others did. He said "Yes ma'm," and "No ma'm," when spoken to. Joanda was very proud of him.

When school was out, they ran almost all the way home. There was so much to tell Mama, and Joanda was homesick for Lolly. She hadn't seen her since morning. But first she must change her dress. She didn't want anything to happen to her pretty red dress.

Coming down the road, Ricky saw Daddy over at the boss-man's barn. Charley Shands had an old barn in the middle of one of the cotton fields, where he kept the tools and machinery used by his sharecroppers and day laborers. Ricky saw Daddy there, working on the boss-man's tractor. Ricky loved a tractor more than anything else in the world.

"I want a ride on Big Charley's tractor," he cried, starting off across the cotton field.

"You've got your good school clothes on," warned Joanda. "Come on home and change them first."

But Ricky did not listen.

Joanda let him go and ran on home. Mama had a big washing on the line and she was taking down the clothes. Lolly was making mud pies in the dirt. She came running and threw herself on her big sister. Joanda hugged and kissed her, then started telling Mama about the lunch.

"*Free* lunch!" exclaimed Mama. "Thinks we're poor, does she?"

"Oh, we can pay if we got the money," said Joanda.

"Well if she thinks . . . what's that? Do you hear Daddy calling yonder? Is that Trouble barking?"

They looked across the field and there by the boss-man's barn, they could see Daddy shouting and waving.

"He wants us," said Mama. "Something's happened." Her face turned white as she ran, stumbling across the cotton rows.

Joanda picked up Lolly and ran too. Once she fell and Lolly fell with her and began to scream. She got up and ran on again. What could have happened? The tractor that had been running and making a loud roaring stood still and silent now. Daddy and Big Charley were bending over something on the ground. Joanda couldn't see Ricky anywhere. Then she heard him whining and wondered if Daddy had spanked him.

When she got there, she saw that Ricky was lying down and Trouble was trying to lick his face. The men stood up and looked at Mama.

"Neva, I've killed him!" said Daddy.

"He ain't killed," said Mama as quiet as could be. "Where'd you hit him at?"

"On his leg," said Daddy.

Mama leaned over and started to pull Ricky's leg back and forth. "Did Daddy hurt you, Ricky?" she asked.

Ricky could talk. "No ma'm," he said, "but *you're* hurtin' me."

"We better take him home," said Mama. "Let's wrap this around him." Over her arm she still had one of Lolly's blankets which she had taken from the clothesline.

"I'll go get a car," said Big Charley.

Mama and Daddy lifted the boy carefully as they could and carried him slowly across the cotton field. Joanda followed with Lolly. Daddy kept telling over and over just how it happened.

"Ricky got up on the tractor behind me, like he always does. Not on the seat—he was standin' on that little platform between the wheels. Then he jumped down without tellin' me and fell over jest as I started to back. I thought he was still on . . . I thought he was still on . . . till I went over a bump, then I shut off the engine quick. I heard a noise like an animal kinda cryin'-like—the roarin' of the tractor was still in my ears. 'Daddy, you run over me,' he kept sayin'; so I hollered for you."

Joanda couldn't bear to hear all the pain in Daddy's voice. It was nobody's fault. Ricky didn't mean to and Daddy didn't mean to. It was just one of those things that nobody could help. It was just one of those things . . . and it happened on Ricky's first day of school. Ricky made such a good start at school and now this.

When they got home, they laid him on the floor of the back porch. In a few minutes Charley Shands came up with J. T. Burgess in Burgess's car. Mrs. Shands was in the back seat. She had been visiting at the Burgesses'.

Joanda held Lolly tight and listened. It got so much worse

[39]

when they all talked about it. They talked on and on about whose fault it was.

"I told Dave not to let his kids play around the barn," said Mrs. Shands.

"The boy's got to go to the hospital," said J. T.

"I'm out of money," said Daddy.

"Won't they let you pay it later?" asked Mama. "We'll make it up somehow. There's still plenty cotton to be pulled, even if we have to go to Missouri to find it. I'll pick my fingers to the bone. . . ."

"The doctor will want some assurance that the bill will be paid, before he even looks at the boy," said Charley Shands firmly.

"But here he is dyin'!" cried Mama. *"Do they let little boys die like this?"*

"Just hush now, Neva," said Daddy. "Don't take on so."

Joanda stepped up. "I still got a dollar and a half," she said. "I was savin' it for Christmas, but I'd rather pay the doctor."

J. T. patted her on the back. "Nobody wants your money, Nannie."

Mrs. Shands turned on Mama. "What have you done with all your cotton money, Neva? You get paid for very pound you pick, besides your own crop. Have you wasted it all in extravagant spending? How do you throw it away so quick?"

Mama was too crushed to answer.

"The doctor and the hospital will want some assurance . . ." Big Charley began again.

"Now, Charley," broke in Mrs. Shands. "You can't advance one penny. I told Dave not to let his kids play around the barn. We're not responsible and they don't need to think we're going to pay for it, even if it was your tractor."

J. T. couldn't stand it any longer.

"I'm takin' this boy to the hospital in my car," he said in a loud voice. "I've got $50 cash in my pocket and they can keep my car if they want more."

"But J. T., how will we . . ." began Mama.

"Now, Neva, don't you worry," said J. T. "*We'll git the money to foot this bill. I'll* git it. The boy's not gonna die —boys don't die of broken legs. He'll git the best of care and he'll git it as long as he needs it."

"Come, Charley, let's go home," said Mrs. Shands.

Big Charley went over to Daddy. "I wish I could help you, Dave . . ."

"Come, Charley," called his wife. The man and woman started across the cotton field toward the barn.

As soon as the Shands were gone, J. T. and Daddy put Ricky flat on the back seat, and Mama sat on the edge of it to hold him. The men rode in front.

Joanda was too stunned to do anything but look. It had all happened so quickly. She watched the car go down the dirt road and turn onto the highway. She followed it with her eyes as long as she could. Lolly slipped out of her arms and ran back to her mud pies. Mavis and Steve came and asked: "Where's Daddy and Mama going?"

Joanda could not tell them.

CHAPTER IV

A Merry Christmas

"Ꮪee, I can walk!"

Ricky raised himself off the bed, walked across it, then slumped awkwardly down again. Trouble jumped up and barked.

"Great stuff!" said Daddy. "We got to git that harness off o' you purty soon."

"You're a turtle in a shell," said Steve, teasing, "with only your head and feet stickin' out. The doctor will git his saw and . . . z-z-z-z-z, he'll saw you in two!"

Ricky laughed. "Will it hurt?"

"It won't hurt half as much to git it off as to keep it on," said Daddy.

Ricky's cast reached from his waist to his toe. He had stayed

in the hospital two weeks and would have to go back again to
have the cast removed. Now he spent most of his time in the
bed in the middle room, where he could see and hear all that
went on in the kitchen. But he was tired of lying down and
anxious to walk again.

Ricky liked to talk about his stay in the hospital. That evening—the day before Christmas—he began at supper to tell it
all over.

"I liked that nurse," he said. "Her name was Miss Whiz-
zengeberry . . . or somethin' like that."

Mama and the children laughed.

"And her hair was so purty, it was *blue* . . ."

"Blue!" cried Mavis. "Do you mean blonde or brunette?"

"Blue!" insisted Ricky.

"BLUE!" repeated Lolly, climbing up on Mama's lap.

"And she brought me two packs of chewing gum and I
chewed them both at the same time," said Ricky.

"My! It must be fun to break your leg and go to the hospital," laughed Steve. "Guess I'll let Big Charley's tractor run
over *my* leg!"

"*What did you say, Steve?*" An unexpected voice broke
into the family chatter. The Hutleys hadn't heard a car honk
in front or anybody call—the usual custom to announce an
arrival. But suddenly, there stood Mrs. Shands just inside the
back kitchen door. She had a large package in her arms. In
a moment, the warmth and happiness of the family meal was
rudely shattered.

"Did you say you'd like Big Charley's tractor to run over
you too, Steve?" Mrs. Shands' voice sounded icy cold. Joanda
shivered.

Nobody could answer a word. But at once, Daddy got up politely and offered Mrs. Shands his chair. She laid her package on the table and sat down.

"I brought you a goose for Christmas," she said.

Still nobody could say a word. They couldn't tell her they didn't want her goose, but they honestly didn't.

"How are you off for groceries, Neva?" Mrs. Shands went on. "Are you having a big Christmas dinner tomorrow? Got a lot of your kinfolk coming?"

"No ma'm," said Mama gently. "We ain't got much, but we'll make out."

After Mama said these words, things felt a little easier. Steve and Mavis got up from their chairs and hurried out. Joanda picked Lolly up and held her tight.

"How's Ricky's leg coming along?" asked Mrs. Shands, walking into the next room.

It sounded as if she meant to be kind, so Mama told her they hoped to get the cast taken off next week.

"That'll feel good, won't it, Ricky?" said Mrs. Shands. "You're tired of staying in bed, I'm sure. But you won't play around the barn any more, will you?"

"No *ma'm*," said Ricky.

Mrs. Shands and Mama went back to the kitchen. Joanda felt better. It was just a friendly Christmas call, after all. The boss-man's wife usually brought something at Christmas time.

As she passed through the kitchen, Mrs. Shands opened the door of the kitchen cabinet. Its shelves were nearly bare.

"Where are your groceries, Neva?" she asked.

Mama's eyes fell. "We're about out," she said nervously. "But we got a little flour and meal and some beans left. And I still got some canned tomatoes and Carnation milk."

"What are you going to have for your Christmas dinner?" asked Mrs. Shands.

"Your goose, I reckon," said Mama with a half-smile.

"But if I hadn't brought it . . ?"

"Great Northern beans!" Mama laughed as she mentioned the well-known brand, the stand-by of the cotton people.

For a moment, Joanda thought that Mrs. Shands would understand and not be critical. Then she saw a flash in the visitor's eyes and she knew her hope was a vain one. Everything was always somebody's fault and soon Mrs. Shands began:

"Won't you folks ever learn? You made good money from

your own cotton and from picking other people's cotton, but what did you do with it? Didn't you buy your winter's supply of flour, meal, lard, sugar and beans with your cotton money?"

"We got some," said Mama meekly, "but not enough to last out the winter."

"It's true what they say," Mrs. Shands went on, "the cotton farmer lives out of a paper sack. Buying that expensive baloney to eat out in the cotton field; never cooking properly, never taking care of a garden or eating green vegetables. No wonder you all get sick."

Mama made no comment. Once Mrs. Shands got started, there was nothing Mama could do to stop her.

"Look how you sharecroppers move every year. If a man's no good, he moves because nobody wants him. If he's good and tries to better himself, he won't stay a cropper long—he'll start to work for himself and so he moves too." She paused. "How will you keep warm this winter?"

"We bought a little coal," said Mama, "but I have to use it to cook with. It won't last long."

"See you don't tear off any of the window or door frames for firewood," said Mrs. Shands sharply.

"Where can we git some wood to burn?" asked Mama.

"We don't furnish firewood," said the woman. "We have no woodland. All our land is in cotton. When that coal is gone, what will you do?"

"I could use that old oil stove," said Mama, "if we could buy coal oil."

Daddy came back in the kitchen. He had been listening on

the porch. He had his hat pushed back on his head. That meant he was good and mad.

"I don't guess we'll stay here much longer, Miz Shands," he said.

"Why not? What's wrong?" asked Mrs. Shands quickly.

"A lot of things," said Daddy. "Big Charley's all right to work for. I like him as good as any boss-man I ever had. Big Charley's always ready to do the right thing—if you'd let him, but you won't."

"You sharecroppers are all alike," retorted Mrs. Shands angrily. "You have to move every year—give up the crop and move off. You've been furnished all along, and your crop's not good, so you move off."

"That's about it," said Daddy firmly.

Then Mrs. Shands changed her tone. "You won't leave with the crop still unpicked, will you, Dave? You'll pull the rest, won't you? We're counting on several more bales of cotton this year."

"I don't guess we'll stay much longer, Miz Shands," said Daddy again.

This threat was the only weapon he had. Daddy didn't know where he could get another job, but just to threaten to go, made Mrs. Shands change her tone.

"Charley don't want to lose you, Dave," she said. "Charley says you're a good worker. We're counting on getting at least two more bales . . ."

"It was right good of you to bring us a goose for Christmas dinner," said Daddy, ushering the woman to the door. "We sure do appreciate it."

"I'll send Neva some groceries," said Mrs. Shands. "I never guessed she was that near out or I'd have brought some with me."

All at once Joanda felt sorry for Mrs. Shands. She was backing down so quickly, now that Daddy was showing his proper spirit.

"Oh, don't trouble yourself, Miz Shands, please don't," begged Mama. "We've got a big sack of Great Northern beans and all the kids sure do love 'em. The pot's never empty—I jest keep puttin' more and more beans in."

"I've got some toys for the children out in my car," said Mrs. Shands. She paused, then she added in a low voice: "I'm sorry we couldn't help with that hospital bill for Ricky." It was an apology.

"That's all right," said Daddy. "It was nobody's fault but my own. I'll find a way to pay back J. T."

"Joanda, come out to the car and get the Christmas toys," said Mrs. Shands. "Merry Christmas to all of you."

"Merry Christmas to you and Big Charley," answered Mama and Daddy.

Joanda looked at Mama. "Shall I go?"

"Yes, go get 'em," said Mama.

Joanda went to the car and Mrs. Shands handed her a large basket full of packages tied with bright ribbons. The girl tried to thank her, but the words stuck in her throat.

"Merry Christmas!" called Mrs. Shands as she drove off.

"Merry Christmas, Miz Shands!" gulped Joanda. *No matter what they do to you,* she thought, *you have to wish everybody a Merry Christmas.*

She hurried in with the packages.

"What's in 'em? Let's open 'em," cried Ricky.

"Put 'em on the dresser in the front room till tomorrow," said Mama. Then she went on talking to Daddy: "Why do we have to move every year? Where can we find another house?"

"There's plenty of sharecroppers' houses empty right now," said Daddy. "Everybody's been movin' the last few weeks."

"There's plenty houses empty," said Mama, "but not fitten to live in. Seems like I've lived in every cropper house in Oak Hollow and Delta Flats and I know. This house ain't near big enough, but it's got a good roof that don't leak. And Big Charley's a good man to work for—the best-hearted boss-man you ever had. You can't go off with part of his crop unpicked. You wouldn't do that to Big Charley."

"Look what he done to me—never offered me a penny to help pay Ricky's doctor bill," said Daddy.

"I been studyin' about that ever since it happened," said Mama. "Maybe he just *couldn't.*"

"Couldn't, huh! Why, Charley Shands is rich, he's made of money," said Daddy. "He couldn't own a thousand acres of this expensive cotton land and have sharecroppers and tenants if he wasn't. He jest didn't want to help me, that's all."

Joanda could keep still no longer. "Does Christmas always mean we gotta move? Are we gonna move right away?"

Mama laughed and that made Daddy laugh too.

"Not by a long sight," said Mama.

"Not before Christmas, you bet!" added Daddy.

The dog came tearing in, barking loudly. Mavis peeked through the back door. "Where is she, the old sour-puss?"

Steve called, "Is she gone?"

"Yes, she's gone," answered Joanda.

"But she left a lot of presents," called Ricky from his bed.

"Can we come in and put up the tree?" asked Steve.

"Gentle Annie!" exclaimed Mama. "What you got there? A holly tree? What's that ole dead limb for?"

"Ain't no real Christmas trees growin' round here," said Mavis. "So we jest cut a little cypress down by the by-o, and we're gonna fix it up purty."

"Goody, goody! We got a tree!" chanted Ricky. "It's gonna be Christmas after all."

Mavis had bought a roll of green crêpe paper at the dime store. She brought it out from its hiding place under the bed, and cut the paper in strips one inch wide. The children sat down and wrapped it around every branch and twig until the tree was a beautiful bright green. It took a long time. Then they set the tree up on a box in the front room by the bed.

"What will we trim it with?" asked Steve.

"I had a mind to buy some of them shiny balls at the five and ten," said Mama, "But I never thought we'd be havin' a tree."

Daddy looked out the open front door. "I don't see a thing but tin cans," he said, laughing. "Couldn't we tie on a few?"

Joanda looked thoughtful for a moment. Then she said: "I've got an idea. We'll make some shiny things to hang on it. It'll be jest a few little ole play-purties like. Mama, where's the can-opener?"

"In the top drawer of the kitchen-cabinet, if Lolly ain't carried it off," said Mama. "How you gonna trim a tree with a can-opener?" The family laughed.

Mama cleared the supper dishes off the kitchen table and Joanda and Steve brought tin cans in from the yard. With the can-opener they cut the round tops and bottoms off the cans. They punched nail holes in the circles of tin and tied strings in the holes to hang them up. Joanda stuck some of the red tomato label pictures onto the rounds of tin. With Mama's heavy old scissors she cut star and heart shapes from the sides of cans.

Meanwhile Daddy had found several ears of popcorn and popped it on the kitchen stove. Mavis strung it on a long string and they hung that up too. Soon the tree was sparkling with silver and bright color. Ricky and Lolly clapped their hands to see it. Even with the front door shut and only one window in the dark room, it looked shiny and beautiful.

"It's purty enough for some of our kinfolk to see," said Mama, "if only they lived near enough to come."

On Christmas morning, Mama got up and started the kitchen fire early. She knew it would take a long time to cook the goose, because it was an old one and tough.

"When will we eat?" the children kept asking.

"When the goose gits tender," Mama answered.

The hours passed, the goose simmered and stewed, but each time Mama poked a fork in it, it was still tough.

"We'll wait a little longer, so it will taste a little better," said Mama, and afterwards they were glad they did.

At last Mama got out her linen tablecloth, the one she had when she was first married, and spread it on the kitchen table. She lengthened the table and put on an extra plate.

"Who's coming, Mama?"

"No one that I know of," she answered. "But when I was a little girl, we always set an extra place at our Christmas table —for the uninvited guest. My Mama's idea was that we should be willing to share even the little we had with whoever might come along."

"Even if it was a wicked tramp?" asked Ricky.

"Yes," said Mama.

"Even if it was a bad man, a cattle rustler?" asked Steve.

"Or a cotton rustler?" asked Daddy.

"Yes," said Mama.

"Or an old colored woman?" asked Joanda.

"Or the Queen of England?" asked Mavis.

"Or a ghost?" put in Ricky.

"Or a big old BEAR?" added Lolly.

Mama nodded yes to all. "What a funny meal we'd have if they *all* came!" Everybody laughed.

The dinner was roast goose and beans and stewed tomatoes and bread. Mama put everything on the table and they all sat down. Even Ricky was propped up on a chair. All at once a car horn sounded in front and they could hear a man's voice calling, "*Hello! Hello!*" Trouble began to bark.

Daddy went out through the front of the house, almost stumbling over the Christmas tree in his hurry.

"Here comes the big old bear!" cried Lolly, pointing her finger.

The car was an old Ford, and the man at the wheel was old too, and alone. He had a long beard and was shabbily dressed. They did not know him.

[52]

"Are you Dave Hutley?" he asked.

"That's right, sir," said Daddy.

"Is that your wife and family?" The man pointed to the others standing at the door.

"That's right, sir," said Daddy again. "We're jest sittin' down to Christmas dinner, sir. We'd be proud to have you eat with us. We ain't got much, but what we got you're plumb welcome to."

"Thank ye kindly," said the man. "I'm a-comin' right in."

He drove his car up to the porch, and followed Daddy and the barking dog into the house. Daddy went to the kitchen and the strange man came too. He sat down at the extra place, and after the others were seated, he said a long grace made up of flowery words. Then he took a look around the table, ending with Mama.

"Are you the uninvited guest?" piped up Ricky.

"I sure am!" The old man roared with laughter. "Now I know I'm in the right house, Neva." He winked at Mama.

Mama said, "You're Uncle Shine Morse. I'd a knowed you sooner except for them whiskers. You didn't have 'em when I was a little girl. Children, I told you Christmas is the day when your kinfolk come. This is my Uncle Shine and yours too."

Daddy got up and shook hands. "Pleased to meet you, sir," he said.

Soon the plates were piled high and everyone was eating. Uncle Shine ate and talked. He said he had traveled all over the country. He had tried everything. He had peddled light-ning rods, painted houses, repaired machines, traded mules and

done all kinds of jobs. Now he was tired of roaming and had come back to Arkansas where he had been born and raised.

"I want to see it again—the cotton country I ran away from."

They talked about Mississippi County and cotton growing. Uncle Shine asked Daddy how he was getting along, and Daddy told how discouraged he was, and how he was always in debt. Mama told how they'd been moving every year since they were first married, and Daddy told about Ricky's accident. "Seems like everything happens to us," he added.

"Too bad," said Uncle Shine. "Looks like you got to pull yourself up by your own bootstraps."

"Bootstraps?" said Daddy. "I don't wear boots. I wear shoes."

"Looks like you got to learn to *save*," Uncle Shine went on.

"Save what?" asked Daddy. "You mean *money?* We never have no money to save."

"*Save?*" echoed young Steve. "We don't have to save. Any time we want money, Daddy can git it from the boss-man."

"It's as easy as that, is it, son?" asked Uncle Shine.

"Oh sure, everybody gits a 'furnish'—even the tenants," explained Steve.

"The boys learn it mighty young," said Uncle Shine.

"He's right, sir," said Daddy. "Steve knows what he's talkin' about."

"And everybody pays 8% interest on the loan, and they don't even know that's high," said Uncle Shine. "I still say you got to save and git a place of your own."

Daddy laughed. "Once a sharecropper, always a sharecropper."

[56]

"Not if you own your team and tools, and git yourself a tractor."

Daddy laughed harder than ever. "You're talkin' about the *moon*," he said. But Mama remembered what Mrs. Shands had said: If a sharecropper's no good, he moves because nobody wants him. If he's good and tries to better himself, he won't stay a cropper long—he'll start to work for himself.

They got up from the table and went into the front room, where the children opened Mrs. Shands's packages. There was a little bear on wheels for Lolly to pull and a toy tractor for Ricky; a tie for Daddy, socks for Steve and handkerchiefs for Mama and the girls. There was a sack of nuts and another of oranges and apples.

"Somebody's comin'," said Mama. "I hear a car outside."

The door opened and in came the Burgesses, all of them. Uncle Shine had to be introduced and everybody had to say *Merry Christmas* to everybody else. They all said how pretty the tree was. Then they stood quiet, while J. T. pulled something out of his pocket.

The Hutleys stared with big eyes. It was a bill-fold. J. T. opened it and brought out a fat roll of bills.

"Money! He's got money!" yelled Ricky from the bed.

"It's a hundred and fifty dollars, Dave," said J. T. "Guess where it came from."

"Must have fell from heaven," said Daddy. "Likely there's a Santa Claus after all."

"It came from your neighbors, Dave," said J. T. "They all knew what a hole you were put in by that big hospital bill, and they wanted to help. Some gave a little, some gave a lot, each gave what he could."

"We only been in this house a year and the folks round here think that much of us?" asked Mama.

"They sure do," said J. T.

Uncle Shine put his arm around Mama's waist.

"They wouldn't a done it, if it hadn't been for you, J. T.," said Daddy in a shaky voice. "Put it right back in your own pocket, to pay yourself back for that hospital loan. If you hadn't a done it . . ." He looked at Ricky.

Ricky was standing up on the bed.

"Now I'm all paid for!" shouted the boy. "Merry Christmas!"

CHAPTER V

Shiny Floors

"I don't want to go, Mama."

Joanda pulled her coat together and buttoned the buttons carefully. She tied a scarf around her head. It was cold outside. It had snowed the night before, and the ground was white. She wished she had warm mittens to wear.

"Tell her the coal's gone and we have to have some wood," called Mama from the bed in the middle room. "Or if she'll send over some coal oil, we can use that. Tell her I got to keep warm or my cold will git worse, and Lolly's too."

"Yes ma'm," said Joanda.

"Take her her basket and thank her nice for the Christmas presents."

"Yes ma'm," said Joanda. She took a deep breath, picked up the empty basket and went out the back door.

[59]

Joanda walked across the cotton field on the path to the boss-man's barn. She looked inside but no one was there. She saw the tractor under the roof, and cultivators, plows and two combines sitting outside. She went on, following the wagon road to the Shands' house, which stood on the next crossroad south.

A cutting wind swept across the low flat fields and set the dry cotton stalks rattling. Joanda wondered how it would feel to be warm all the way through. She felt sorry for Steve and Mavis. They were out in the cold flats, helping Daddy pull cotton. They had to wear gloves to pull boll and all. But she'd rather pull cotton even on the coldest winter day than do what she had to do now. Mama and Lolly were sick and getting sicker, so she just had to do it.

Joanda had been to the Shands' house only once before. It was in the spring during a rainy spell. She would never forget that, for she had walked in the mud and her shoes were muddy. She couldn't remember what she went for. All she remembered were the shiny floors and the mud tracks she made on them. She would never forget how Mrs. Shands had scolded her for tracking in mud.

There was no mud now. All the ground was frozen hard. But the snow stuck to her shoes. It might make tracks. She must not forget to brush all the snow off her shoes before she went in.

It was hard to ask a favor of Mrs. Shands, but Lolly was so sick. Only their desperate need could make her go. Lolly, who was always bouncing and bubbling over with life, lay sick and listless now. Each time she stirred, she cried and moaned. Mama wouldn't let Joanda hold her, because Joanda might catch her cold and get down sick too.

She thought of Uncle Shine and wondered what had become of him. He had made them so happy on Christmas, and hopeful too, although he had done nothing but visit. He had come—and gone. He didn't tell them where he was staying or whether he would come back. Joanda wished she knew where to find him. Your own kinfolk were always ready and willing to help. But she couldn't count on him now. She must go on. She walked more slowly as she came closer.

The Shands' house was a one-story bungalow, painted white. Shrubs and rose-bushes were planted on the lawn in front, all covered up now with snow. A chicken yard, garage and small barn were at the back; also a pump-house over the well, to pump water to the bathroom inside.

Joanda walked quickly along the cement walk that led from the driveway to the back door. She must not stop or her courage would fail. She knocked briskly, then leaned over and brushed the snow off her shoes with her fingers. She stamped her feet on the cement step. Looking up, she saw that the sky was heavy with black clouds. It was going to snow again.

She expected a prompt answer to her knock, but none came. Likely Mrs. Shands was away—but no, the garage doors were closed. Their car must be there, and she had noticed smoke coming out of the chimney.

She knocked again and waited. Likely Mrs. Shands had run over to one of her neighbors. The thought made Joanda feel easier, but she knew it only postponed her errand. She would have to come back again, and the second time would be harder.

It must be nice to live in a big house like this. But those shiny floors, with all that wax on them, would never do. Daddy and Steve and Ricky would keep them tracked up with mud and snow. Linoleum was better—it was easier. You could mop up the tracks in a jiffy.

Courageously, Joanda knocked the third time, forgetting her fears.

Then she heard movements inside. Mrs. Shands was at home after all. Before the girl had time to be scared, the door opened and the woman stood there.

She looked so different, Joanda hardly knew her. She wasn't dressed in stylish clothes or hat. She had on an apron, as soiled as if it were Mama's. Her hair was mussed and her face was red as if she had been crying.

"Oh, it's you, Joanda," she said.

"Yes ma'm, I brought your basket back," said Joanda. "Thank you for all the Christmas presents. We sure did appreciate them."

"Come in out of the cold, Joanda," said Mrs. Shands.

She took the basket and set it on the table. The kitchen was warm. A coal fire was burning in the stove.

Even the woman's voice was different. It sounded tired and unhappy. She never once looked at the girl's shoes to see if there was snow on them. She didn't look at the shiny floors, to see if the girl's shoes had made tracks on them. She led the way to the front room and said, "Sit down, won't you?"

Joanda sat down. She sat on a purple couch. It was just like the one in Atkins' furniture store window in town, with the price-tag that said *Davenport $99.98*. It was much bigger than the one Mama had picked out. It was so soft, Joanda sank down into the seat and breathed deeply.

Mrs. Shands' front room was beautiful. It was so beautiful it took the girl's breath away. It had pretty flowered wall-paper on the walls, and there were pictures hanging up. It had lace curtains at the windows and velvet carpet on the floor. Joanda wished she were barefooted so she could feel the soft-ness of the velvet carpet with her toes. Suddenly she shivered.

"Are you cold?" asked Mrs. Shands. "Come and sit by the oil heater. We just got this new one put in. It heats the whole house—except the kitchen—like a furnace. But it's not paid for yet . . ."

"Not paid for?" echoed Joanda.

She moved to a straight chair by the big box-like heater and held out her cold hands.

"No," said Mrs. Shands. Her eyes filled with tears and she looked as if she might cry again.

Joanda got that strange feeling she had had at the back door. This was a different Mrs. Shands, one she had never seen be-fore. There was nothing stuck-up about her.

"How are you folks getting along?" asked Mrs. Shands in a dull voice.

Joanda tried to remember the things Mama had told her to say.

"Mama said she hated to send the basket back empty," ex-plained Joanda, "but we jest didn't have a thing to put in it."

"Why should you?" asked Mrs. Shands.

"Mama says it's always polite to put a little something in a basket or a plate when you return it," said Joanda.

[63]

"Oh, I see," said Mrs. Shands. "But you didn't have a thing."

"We've got quite a lot of flour in the flour can," said Joanda cheerfully. It was easier to talk to Mrs. Shands than she had expected it would be. "And I could have made a batch of biscuits, if Mama had told me just how to do it . . . I did it once before and they were good, too. I could have put a few biscuits in the basket for you, but . . ."

"Oh, that's all right," said Mrs. Shands. "Don't give it another thought."

"We wanted to return your courtesy, but . . ."

"Yes, I understand," interrupted Mrs. Shands. Then she said abruptly, and somewhat bitterly: "Your daddy hasn't moved out, then."

"No, but as soon as he can find a house fitten to live in . . ."

Mrs. Shands suddenly began to cry. She sank down in the

overstuffed couch, put her hands over her face and began to sob. Joanda stood up and stared at her. She had never seen the boss-man's wife cry before, and she could not believe her own eyes. She just stood and looked.

Then a revelation came to her.

This woman, who had always seemed so hard and cold and icy, was just like any one else underneath. This woman, who had scolded and found fault with Daddy and Mama and blamed them for all their troubles, had troubles of her own. She must have dreadful troubles, or she would not be crying like this.

Joanda ran to her and put her arms around her. She felt just the way she did whenever Lolly hurt herself. She wanted to comfort her. She felt so sorry for her she wanted to cry too. Then she knew she must not cry. Mrs. Shands needed help and there was nobody but Joanda, a little girl of ten, to help her.

The next minute Mrs. Shands was telling her troubles.

"If your daddy leaves, Charley won't be able to pay his debts . . ."

"You got debts?" asked Joanda, her eyes wide with surprise. "I thought only sharecroppers had debts. Big Charley's the boss-man, he owns lots of farms, he's *rich!*"

"Everybody's in debt in the cotton country," said Mrs. Shands.

"Even the owners?" asked Joanda.

"Even the owners," said Mrs. Shands.

"Even the *rich* owners who've got combines and mechanical cotton-pickers?" asked Joanda.

"It takes years to pay for that expensive machinery," said

Mrs. Shands. "Our land payments are already past due, so the furniture has to wait." She looked about the room. "That heater's not paid for, this davenport, my electric refrigerator . . . If your daddy goes before he gets the crop out, and other tenants leave, we can't make the land payments. Charley still owes on his tractor, too."

Joanda began to understand. "So that's why Big Charley couldn't help with Ricky's hospital bill," she said slowly.

"Yes," said Mrs. Shands. "He wanted to, but I wouldn't let him. I knew about all these other payments he had to meet. He's so easy-going, somebody has to be businesslike. Do you know why they call him *Big* Charley?"

"Daddy said it was because he's a big-hearted man to work for," said Joanda, smiling.

"Yes," said Mrs. Shands. "And because he's always biting off more than he can chew. He'd give away his last dime . . ."

"But ain't that what money's for?" asked the girl. "Daddy can't keep his money either."

"You have to pay your debts and save something over, if you ever want to have security," said Mrs. Shands. "But that's too much to hope for in the cotton country."

"*You* don't want us to go then?" asked Joanda. "And Big Charley don't?"

"We need you," said Mrs. Shands simply. "We need a big family like yours, with three or four children for extra hands. Without you, we can't get out our crop. We're dependent on you. We need you."

"Here we thought you wanted to get shet of us," said Joanda, surprised. "And now you say you need us."

"Yes," said Mrs. Shands, drying her eyes. "If we could get two more bales or maybe three of the pulled cotton, it would help a lot."

"Daddy and Steve and Mavis are pulling every day now," said Joanda. "I'll tell Daddy not to move this year because the boss-man needs us."

Mrs. Shands smiled bitterly. "Does your daddy always take your advice?"

"I think he will," said Joanda simply. "Mama wants to stay because the roof don't leak. She says we're lucky to have a dry house, even if it's not warm."

"Not warm? What do you mean?"

"Daddy and Steve and Mavis put on all the clothes they got and they keep warm workin' in the field," explained Joanda. "And Ricky and me, we're warm when we go to school. It's worst for Mama and Lolly, they've got to stay in the house all the time. That's how they got their colds."

"Colds? They're sick?"

"They been in bed for a week, but it's warm in bed. We got heavy covers."

"Who looks after them?"

"I do," said Joanda with pride. "I can cook . . . when there's a fire in the stove."

"What do you do when there's no fire?"

"Eat cold stuff."

Mrs. Shands stood up. "Why didn't you tell me?" Her voice sounded angry. "They're sick and the coal's all gone and the groceries are used up." She remembered the nearly-empty kitchen cabinet shelves at Christmas time.

"Big Charley may have plenty of debts to pay," said his wife, "but he'll always be big-hearted. He won't stand for anything like this."

"But our 'furnish' don't begin till March," protested Joanda. "Mama said we had to squeeze along till then."

"Your 'furnish' begins ahead of time this year, if you stay with us," said Mrs. Shands. "It begins right here and now. I'll get my car out and drive you home. We'll stop at Brownie's Country Store on our way. Charley's credit's always good. I've wasted too much time this morning crying and feeling sorry for myself. I'll just fix myself up a little." She disappeared in the bedroom.

A little later Mrs. Shands and Joanda went out the back door hand in hand. It was snowing heavily, but Joanda was warmed through and through.

*   *   *

When they reached the shotgun house with a load of groceries and a large can of coal oil, Joanda was worried for fear Mama and Lolly might be worse, she had stayed away so long. Then she saw a car in front, and when she and Mrs. Shands went in, Mrs. Burgess met them at the door.

The house was warm. The stove had a hot coal fire in it and a pot of beans was cooking.

"I'd a been over sooner," Aunt Lessie said, "but I was in bed with a cold myself. I looked down the road this morning and when I saw there wasn't any smoke coming out of Neva's chimney, I knew something was wrong. I had J. T. bring some coal over right away."

Joanda hurried into the bedroom. Lolly sat up in bed, held out her arms and cried, "Nannie, Nannie." The girl picked her up and held her close.

"I brought all the medicine I had in the house," said Mrs. Burgess, "and I think both my patients are better already."

Joanda could hardly wait to talk to Mama.

"Miz Shands said they got debts too, Mama," she said.

"You mean they owe *money?*" Mama couldn't sit up yet, but she did look better.

Mrs. Shands came in. "We sure do, Neva. Our land's not paid for. We're always in debt."

"Always in debt?" Mama couldn't believe it.

"Sure," said Mrs. Shands. "Everybody that fools with cotton is in debt to somebody else. The sharecropper's in debt to the tenant, the tenant to the owner, the owner to the gin, the

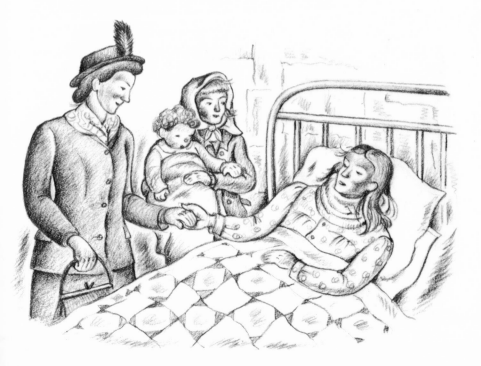

gin to the bank, the bank to . . . whoever's at the top, and probably he's in debt to the Lord."

Mama stared.

"So we all spend our lives workin' off our debts," she said slowly, "and we never git 'em paid."

"That's right," said Mrs. Shands.

"Then we're all in the same boat." Mama smiled at Mrs. Shands and Mrs. Shands smiled back.

"So you got your worries too," Mama said. "I always thought only sharecroppers had troubles."

"Mama," broke in Joanda, "Miz Shands has got a new purple couch, like the kind you want. It's so big and soft and squnchy, you sink right down on it, and it feels so good. But *it's not paid for!* If we don't git the rest of the cotton crop out for the boss-man, they'll have to let it go back to Atkins' furniture store. They need us to help them!"

"It'd be a shame to lose a nice davenport like that," said Mama. She paused. "I can see now why Big Charley couldn't help us with Ricky's hospital bill. I kept studyin' about that and I says to Dave likely he *couldn't,* and I was right."

Mrs. Shands nodded. She couldn't speak.

"Can't you git Daddy to stay?" asked Joanda, jiggling Lolly up and down, "when they need us so bad?"

"He'll stay," said Mama.

"Then your troubles are over, Miz Shands," said Joanda.

The woman put an arm around the girl's shoulder. "Thank you, Nannie."

She turned to Mama. "I know you folks don't have it easy and I intend to help you more. But remember, there's plenty of trouble to go around. Old Man Trouble don't miss any-body. He knocks on everybody's door, rich and poor alike."

"I never thought of it that-a-way," said Mama softly. "I'm sure glad you told me."

From that moment the two women were friends.

Woof! Woof! barked the dog.

Joanda laughed. "Mama, there's Trouble at the door wantin' in!"

*   *   *

A few days later, Big Charley came and had a good talk with Dave Hutley, who agreed to stay. Big Charley promised him day labor while out of crop. Then he added: "You're too good a worker, Dave, to stay a sharecropper. You try to get your own tools and mules and I promise you—the first tenant house empty on my place, I'll let you have it."

CHAPTER VI

The Library Book

"Mr. Bonehead was just a dummy, made of wood," said the boys.

"He walked and he talked!" said the girls.

There was great excitement at recess. A woman and a man had brought a ventriloquist act to school, and all the children were talking about it.

"That lady, Madame Simonds, made him walk by winding up something in the back," said Jolene Burgess.

"She made him talk by moving her own lips, only you couldn't see her do it," added Shirley Mason.

"Oh, I've heard lots of that stuff over the radio," said one of the boys.

"But it's better to see it—a wooden dummy talking," said Bug Burgess.

"He sure did look real," said Joanda.

"How could he cry when he was made of wood?" asked Ricky. He was out of his cast now and back at school again.

"Likely she had a rubber ball with water in it," said Shirley, "and she squirted it."

The children laughed.

"But how did he know everybody's names?" asked Joanda.

"Oh, Steve told her when he helped her unload her truck this morning," said Mavis. "I saw him pointing out different kids to her."

"Look! Here they come!"

The children ran to the door and Madame Simonds came down the steps with her bags and props, and a long roll of stage scenery. The boys ran to help her. Then came her helper, little Mr. Whoozit, carrying the dummy slung over his shoulder. Joanda got a close look at Mr. Bonehead. His eyes and mouth were painted in bright colors on his carved face. He wore a red hat with a long feather, and had on a Mexican coat with sparklers over it. The children reached up to touch the sparklers.

"Are you afraid of him?" Joanda asked Ricky.

"Course not." Ricky poked the dummy's eyes with his fingers. "He don't even wink."

They watched as the man and woman packed their belongings into their car. It had a Texas license.

"Gee! That was the best show I ever saw!" said Ricky. He turned to Joanda, but she had already gone inside.

In the schoolhouse, the hall was empty and quiet.

Joanda went to the bubbler and for the first time took a

drink of water from it. It was better than drinking out of a dipper. She walked down the hall. Quietly she pushed open the swinging door of the new dining room. She had never been inside. No one was there. Mrs. Bronson, the cook, must have stepped out for a minute. So Joanda went in on tiptoe.

There were two long low tables and two higher ones, covered with pretty oil cloth. They had bouquets of flowers in the middle. There were red-checked curtains at the windows and green ferns on the window sills. Big pots of food were simmering on the stove, and the smell was delicious. Joanda wished that she and her brothers and sister could eat there.

Near the stove was a sink, and one of the taps was running. Joanda tiptoed over to turn it off. Then she stopped just in time. She nearly fell over with surprise. Stuffing both hands

over her mouth, she caught herself before she made a sound.

There was Miss Fenton down on her hands and knees under the sink, putting something into a paper sack. She was so busy she did not look up. Joanda stared. She saw what Miss Fenton was picking up. She tiptoed back out as quickly and quietly as she could. She was sure Miss Fenton had not seen her.

After the entertainers drove off, the children settled down to Arithmetic, and then the bell rang for lunch. Joanda thought unhappily of her cold lunch. It was "fried pies" again —she had seen Mama fixing them. She never liked them much. They always made her stomach ache all afternoon, they were so heavy. They were made of left-over biscuit dough, cut in circles by a saucer, then folded over with a few dried, stewed peaches inside, and fried in deep fat. She thought with longing of the appetizing smell in the school dining room.

The hot lunch children filed down the hall, where Mrs. Bronson was soon heaping their plates high. The cold lunch children huddled around the little table in the back of Miss Fenton's room, where their lunches were piled.

Miss Fenton came in hurriedly and seemed excited. She picked up one lunch wrapped in a transparent bread paper. "Whose is this?" she asked. A pale-faced boy called Glenwood claimed it. Miss Fenton opened the paper.

"Why, it's got cockroaches in it!" she exclaimed.

The children jumped back.

"Don't put one on me!" cried Ricky.

Miss Fenton opened a lunch wrapped in newspaper, another in a sugar sack, and finally Joanda's paper sack.

"Why, they've all got cockroaches in them," she said.

[75]

"They're not fit to eat. You'll have to come into the dining room and eat hot lunches today."

She looked at Joanda. "Is Ricky's in the same sack with yours?"

"Yes ma'm," said Joanda, dropping her eyes.

"I wonder how the cockroaches got in here," said Miss Fenton. "We've had plenty in the kitchen. We must buy some roach powder."

It was very funny. Joanda was afraid to look Miss Fenton straight in the eyes for fear she would laugh. Then she knew she must not give Miss Fenton away, for she understood *why* she had done it. Suddenly she was very happy. At last they could eat with the other children.

"COCKROACHES IN THE COLD LUNCHES THIS MORNING!" announced Miss Fenton in a loud voice, as she led the children in.

They were greeted by a chorus of laughter, but a table was ready, so they sat down. Joanda and Ricky were hungry. They each ate two platefuls and they drank all their milk. Miss Fenton was pleased, but what would Mama say?

Still stranger things happened that afternoon. Miss Fenton was an unusual teacher. She was always surprising the children by doing things never done in school before. In Fourth Grade spelling, she asked, "Who knows what *permanent* means?" The children could spell it, but did not know its meaning.

Joanda held up her hand. "It means something that lasts forever."

Miss Fenton was pleased and asked Joanda how she knew.

"I read it in the newspaper." She did not add that the newspaper was pasted upside-down on the wall.

The children used the word in sentences. They talked of *permanent friendships*—friends you know all your life; and of *permanent homes*.

"Do you mean the kind you never move away from?" asked Joanda.

Miss Fenton said yes. Then she mentioned *permanents*, the kind of curl that stays in your hair.

"My Mama's gonna git one next fall," said Joanda, "if we make a good cotton crop."

The children laughed and made Joanda feel ashamed. She wished she hadn't said it.

The rest of the afternoon was given to a Beauty Parlor and Barber Shop party. When the lunch dishes were washed, Mrs. Bronson came in to help. The school nurse arrived in her car, bringing the equipment.

Everybody's hair was to be washed. The nurse used coal oil on some of the heads first, then a sweet-smelling shampoo. Mrs. Bronson was the barber and with her electric clippers soon had the shaggy heads of the boys looking like shorn sheep.

It was fun, and all the children laughed. "Cut mine! Cut mine!" they begged.

Joanda sat on the bench, with Ricky by her side, her hand clutching his tightly, waiting with the others. Because everybody else was doing it, they'd have to do it too. At last their turn came. Mrs. Bronson snipped Ricky and the nurse shampooed Joanada. Then Miss Fenton took a pair of shears and began to cut her hair.

"Oh, *don't!*" Joanada screamed and jumped from her chair.

"You just better not cut my hair, you old teacher, you!" she cried. "My mother didn't say you could do it." Anger changed her pretty face to an ugly one. "I saw what you did! I saw you put those cockroaches in our paper sack! *I saw you!*"

Miss Fenton's face turned red. Fortunately most of the children had already left the room. She ignored the girl's remark completely. She had the nurse explain to Joanda how much easier it is to take proper care of the hair when it is short. Miss Fenton had asked all the mothers' permissions except Joanda's, because Joanda had been absent the day before.

"Since you feel the way you do, I'll just trim off the ends a little." Reluctantly, Joanda sat down. "I'll trim it off even and then put it up in curlers. I have a pretty silk scarf for you to tie over your head, Joanda. You leave the curlers on until

tomorrow morning, and you'll be surprised how pretty your
hair will be—as pretty as a real permanent."

Joanda frowned and did not answer. As she sat there she
grew more and more worried. Mama would see that hers and
Ricky's hair had been cut and Ricky would tell about the hot
lunch. Mama would be mad as hops.

That afternoon, Joanda was afraid to go in the house when
she got home from school. She cut across the cotton field with
Jolene Burgess and went up to their house and played till dark.

Then she came home, opened the front door softly and crept
in. Mama was busy getting supper in the kitchen. Mavis and
Steve were talking about the ventriloquist show and Ricky
was trying to talk like Mr. Bonehead. He must have forgotten
to mention the hot lunch and the barber shop. But why didn't
Mama notice his hair had been cut?

Joanda took her clothes off quietly and slipped into bed.
She covered her head with the quilt. The silk scarf was a
pretty one, bright blue with yellow lilies on it. But Mama
mustn't see it. The curlers hurt her head, but she couldn't help
it. She must leave them on till morning as Miss Fenton had
told her to do.

Ricky came in the bedroom, and seeing a bump in the bed,
punched her.

"Stop it!" she said.

"Nannie's in bed, Mama," said Ricky. "Nannie's gone to
bed without her supper."

"What's the matter?" called Mama. "Don't you feel good?"

"Got the stomach ache," said Joanda. She remembered the
stomach ache she would have had if she'd eaten the fried pies
for lunch.

"Want some castor oil?" called Daddy.

"No, it's not that bad," answered Joanda.

The family laughed.

"Comin' out to supper, Nannie?" called Steve, a little later.

"No, I'm not hungry. Just sleepy."

They let her alone after that. She fell asleep to the murmur of their voices.

Joanda woke up early the next morning. Mama was in the kitchen and had started the fire. Lolly was walking around, climbing up on things and talking. Lolly could say many words now.

Joanda heard the singing of the teakettle and the clatter of the dishes. She smelled the appetizing odors of boiling coffee and sizzling grease. She heard Mama open the oven door to put the biscuits in. Breakfast would soon be ready.

"Git up, you lazy bones!" called Mama.

Joanda heard Lolly say, "I wanna big biscuit with grease gravy and syrup on it. Mama, is the gravy done?"

"It's on the table, now leave it alone like a good girl," said Mama.

Joanda came to the kitchen door as soon as she was dressed and stood watching sleepily. "Lolly," she said, "who likes you best?"

"You do, Nannie," said the little girl.

"Lolly, who's mean to you?" asked Joanda.

"Ever'body's mean to me 'ceptin' Nannie!"

A bucket of water with a dipper in it sat on a chair. Lolly put one foot on the rung of this chair, then stepped with her other foot onto her own chair.

"I'm hungry," she said. "I want gravy quick."

Her foot slipped. As she threw her hand up, she knocked the bowl of hot gravy and spilled it over her hand and arm. She screamed loudly.

Joanda got to her first and pulled her away from the table. Mama ran over and wiped the gravy off with a dish towel.

"She's burned," said Mama. "Git some coal oil quick."

Joanda's hands shook so she could hardly tip the can and pour it. She brought a saucerful to Mama, who dipped the towel and wrapped it around the baby's arm as quickly as she could. All this time Lolly was screaming.

Daddy and the other children had jumped into their clothes and stood looking. "I'll take her to the doctor," Daddy said.

Mama said, "All right, let's go." She started to take Lolly from Joanda's arms, but couldn't. Lolly clung tightly to her sister, crying hard.

"You'll have to go along, Nannie," said Daddy.

"Can't we go too?" asked the other children. "You can drop us off at school on the way back."

"Well, get in," said Daddy.

Mama took the biscuits out of the oven and let them sit to turn cold. Breakfast was forgotten as they climbed into the truck. Joanda and Lolly rode with Mama and Daddy in front, the others in the back. Lolly had quieted down and seemed to be sleeping on Joanda's shoulder.

"Will any doctor be up this early?" asked Mama.

"Which one will we go to?" asked Daddy.

"I don't know," said Mama. "Got any money in your pocket?"

"About fifty cents," said Daddy. "Let's go to a drug store first and ask what's good for a burn. Likely we could git something for fifty cents."

"We'll let the druggist look at it," said Mama, "and if he says she needs a doctor, we'll ask him which one to go to."

Joanda held Lolly while the druggist unwrapped her arm. He said the burn was not serious. He covered the baby's arm with salve and bandaged it. He gave Mama a tube of the salve for fifty cents. Lolly began to talk and laugh on the way home, so they knew she was all right.

Mama didn't notice Joanda's hair until they stopped by the schoolhouse to let the children off.

"What you done to your hair, Nannie?" she asked. "What's that riggin' you're wearin'?"

Joanda answered in a small voice: "Teacher gave me a sort of a permanent. She gave the other girls one too. She asked

all the mothers but you, 'cause I was absent day before yesterday."

"Permanents cost money," said Mama. A hard look came
over her face.

"This one's free," said Joanda, "she said so."

"And she gave you a *free* lunch too," Mama went on.
"Ricky told me. Thinks we're pore, don't she? Hot lunches
and permanents in school! We send you to school to git book-
learnin', to study lessons. I guess I better go in and speak a
piece of my mind to this teacher o' yours."

"Oh Mama, *don't!*" begged Joanda. "She's all right, she's
nice . . . I *like* her . . . she jest does some funny things, that's
all. You can't never tell what she's gonna do next."

But Mama would not listen.

Daddy took Lolly and Mama rushed into the school building, with Joanda and Ricky at her heels. Mavis and Steve
joined a ball game that had already begun. The hall was empty
and no one seemed to be around. Mama turned to Joanda
and whispered nervously, "Where can I find her?"

"We'll have to look," said the girl.

They found Miss Fenton in the dining room, talking to Mrs.
Bronson. She looked up in surprise as Mrs. Hutley came in
followed by her two children. Mama's hair wasn't combed and
she still had her apron on.

"What do you mean by making my children eat a free
lunch?" demanded Mama. "Think we're too pore to pay for
it?"

"Why, Mrs. Hutley," said Miss Fenton, "didn't the children
tell you? We found cockroaches in their cold lunch yester-

day. You wouldn't want them to eat it after that, would you?"

"Why, er . . . I s'pose not . . ." said Mama weakly. Then she began again. "And you gave Nannie a permanent . . ." Mama's bravado was rapidly fading away in these strange surroundings.

"I'll go and comb out Joanda's hair for you to see," said Miss Fenton, "while Mrs. Bronson shows you our new dining room." Joanda and Miss Fenton went out.

Mama looked at the cupboard full of groceries and the pots cooking on the stove. Suddenly her heart smote her—she had been depriving her children of good nourishment to build their bodies and give them strength. The food was better than she could give them at home. She didn't need to be told that. She looked around the pretty room while Mrs. Bronson explained everything.

"I never thought it was nice like this," said Mama. "Maybe they wouldn't get sick so much . . ."

Mrs. Bronson explained that the price of meals was charged for those who had big families and could not pay, and said there were funds to take care of that. No one need know they couldn't pay. She added, "You'll let them come, won't you?"

Mama nodded.

When she returned to Miss Fenton's room, there was Joanda with her hair combed out. It hung soft and naturally to her shoulders.

"I only cut off the stringy ends," said Miss Fenton. "Joanda's so pretty . . ."

"Purty, huh!" sniffed Mama. "She don't look no different from other young uns. I don't want her gittin' notions . . ."

[84]

"She's as pretty as a picture," said Miss Fenton, "and it won't hurt her to know it, either." She turned to a shelf of books at the back of the room. "We're starting a school library. We want to get more story books . . ."

"I thought they come to school to read outa *lesson* books," said Mama.

"Mama, Miss Fenton says I can take a book home with me and read it."

Mama shook her head. "We don't have no truck with books."

"Here's a pioneer story," said Miss Fenton. "You'll like it, Mrs. Hutley, when Joanda reads it to you. She's one of the best readers in the whole school and a prize speller too. She likes words and understands what they mean. She ought to read constantly."

At these words of praise, Mama flushed with pride, all her anger gone. Then she remembered she was keeping Daddy waiting. She thanked Miss Fenton and hurried out.

That evening Joanda ran all the way home. She could hardly wait to read the library book she carried under her arm.

CHAPTER VII

The Glass Door

"Say, this is *good!*" said Joanda.

She was sitting on the back porch when Daddy came up. "What is?"

"It's a book, a pioneer story," said the girl. "I been lookin' at all the pictures. We've got a library at school, with story books to take home and read."

"I told that teacher my kids go to school to study *lesson* books," said Mama at the door.

"Come on in, let's see if I can read it," said Daddy. The children trooped in the house behind him. "Will you tell me the hard words if I get stuck, Nannie?"

"I sure will," said Joanda proudly.

Daddy sat down by the kitchen stove and began to read the book aloud. When he got tired, Joanda took his place. Mama went on getting supper while she listened. The children crowded close. Even Lolly sat very still.

The book told of hard work and courage and struggle. It had happiness, meanness and sorrow in it. At the sad parts they all cried. Daddy and Joanda read each evening after school until the end was reached.

"It sounds like real to me," said Daddy. "I feel like I know them folks somehow."

"That's 'cause they're just like us. They had the same troubles in them days too," said Mama. "We're not the only ones had it hard."

Spring had come to the cotton country and it began to rain every day. The dirt roads became mud-puddles and the banks of the ditches and bayous were running full. Daddy drove the children to school in the truck. Then one morning he was afraid he would stick the truck, so the children started for school on foot.

They had finished reading the library book the night before and Joanda was taking it back.

Joanda never knew just how it happened. Afterwards she wished she hadn't tried to lift Ricky over the mud-puddle. But he had no rubbers and she did. When she was halfway across, the book slipped out from under her arm.

"Oh! Oh!" she cried. Then she dropped Ricky and he got his feet muddy and wet, after all.

But it was the book that mattered. Joanda had told Miss Fenton she would take good care of it. Daddy had folded a newspaper around its beautiful blue cloth covers, so not a spot should get on them. He had turned the pages carefully. Each time after they finished reading, Mama had put the precious book up on a high shelf out of Lolly's reach. Joanda wanted to be sure to return the book to school as pretty and clean as when she borrowed it.

Now it had fallen in the mud-puddle. Horror-stricken, she reached down through the cold, slimy mud and brought it up. She held it out at arm's length.

"By golly, you'll ketch it!" cried Ricky. "Teacher will sure whoop the buttons off your dress for *that!*"

"I'm goin' home," said Joanda. "You go on to school. Hurry and you can ketch up with Steve and Mavis. They're waitin' at the corner."

Joanda walked slowly back, staring at the book, her heart sick within her. The whole family had loved every word and picture in the book and now she had ruined it. She knew Daddy hadn't any money to buy a new one to take its place.

They were living on borrowed "furnish" now. She tried to open the pages which were stuck together with mud, but it was impossible. She stopped and thought awhile. She couldn't take the book home and she couldn't take it back to school.

She cut across the field, went to the top of the bayou bank and threw the book as far as it would go. It landed in the middle of the stream. She watched it slowly sink from sight.

The bayou was deep. She could never get the book again.

Then, panic-stricken, she ran home.

Back in the house, she sat down on a chair beside the stove. Mama questioned her, but all she said was: "I can't go to school any more."

Mama and Daddy decided she was sick and let her alone. It began to rain again. Daddy talked about the rain as he, too, sat by the stove.

"The field is a loblolly," he said. "If this keeps on, we'll never git the cotton planted. We ought to been breakin' ground two weeks ago. Most years we'd have our plowin' done by now."

"I was over to Lessie's yesterday," said Mama. "That gumbo mud gits on her chickens' feet and makes balls so big they can't walk. She has to ketch each one and knock the mud off."

"Why, when you walk in it yourself," said Daddy, "your feet git as big as a nail-keg! It takes you three hours to walk a mile and a quarter!"

He laughed, but Joanda didn't. Her face still had that stricken look.

"But gumbo land is best for cotton," Daddy went on. "It holds the moisture longer."

Mama looked out the window. "If it don't stop rainin', the house will soon be floatin' in water."

"Glad we don't live no nearer to Pemiscot by-o," said Daddy. He pronounced the word *bayou:* by-ō. "Them folks might have to git out in boats."

The days passed and it kept on raining. Joanda helped about the house and took care of Lolly. One day she made her a pair of jeans out of Steve's old pants. When she tried them on her, the girl brightened up and said, "She sure does look sweet with 'em on," and hugged and kissed her.

When Miss Fenton sent word home by Mavis, inquiring about the library book, Joanda refused to answer. Daddy and Mama both questioned her, but she told nothing. Mavis was unable to report to Miss Fenton, for the road got so bad, none of the children could get to school. And there was no work Daddy could do. So they all sat around in the house and waited for better weather.

"I sure wish you'd a brought us another of them good story books to read, Nannie," said Daddy. "It would make the time go faster."

Joanda frowned and said nothing.

At last the rain stopped, the sky cleared and the children started back to school. All but Joanda, who refused to go. Mama couldn't make her, so, in her easy-going way, said nothing and let her stay at home.

"Why, Joanda," said Aunt Lessie Burgess, dropping in one day. "Why ain't you in school where you belong?"

Joanda dropped her eyes. "I don't like school."

"The road's too muddy," hastily explained Mama.

"But the other children walk," said Aunt Lessie. "It's not too muddy for them."

"She ain't got rubbers or galoshes that fit her right," said Mama.

"I'll send over some old ones of the twins'," said Aunt Lessie. "They've outgrown them and they ought to be jest right for her."

"Don't you bother," said Mama. "She jest *don't like* this school."

"But I thought she liked it so much," said Aunt Lessie. "She was the best reader and the best speller, too, the twins told me."

"It's the teacher," said Mama. "She jest can't stand her."

"Why, all the kids are crazy about Miss Fenton," said Aunt Lessie. "Jolene and Arlene say they'd rather have her than Miss Tyler, but Miss Tyler's good too. We've got the two best teachers we ever had at Delta Flats School this year."

"She does mighty funny things, that teacher does," Mama went on. "I never heard of such goin's on in any school before —this washin' their heads and cuttin' their hair and feedin' 'em we don't know what. And there's another thing. She don't learn 'em out of lesson books, she's gittin' story books . . ."

"They can learn out of them too," said Aunt Lessie. "Times are changing. The schools ain't what they used to be, but Miss Fenton's all right."

"Did you hear what she done?" asked Mama in a low voice. "*She put cockroaches in the cold lunch sacks.*"

Aunt Lessie chuckled. "Oh, I don't believe that."

"But Joanda saw her with her own eyes," said Mama.

"Did you, Joanda?" asked Aunt Lessie.

Joanda stared at the floor. She couldn't answer the question. She wished she hadn't told anybody, but Mama had pulled it out of her somehow. She wished the women would stop talking about her.

"Is it any wonder she hates her and won't go back to school any more?" said Mama.

"Well, she better forget it and go," said Aunt Lessie briskly. "Nannie's too smart a girl to be sittin' around here all day long doin' nothing. All the children are better off in school, now they got that hot lunch and everything up-to-date. My twins are fleshnin' up, they eat so much."

After the rains were over, the spring work began with a rush. As soon as the fields dried off, Daddy started working long hours, driving Big Charley's tractor, breaking ground. He came home barely long enough to eat and sleep.

One day after the roads were passable, a car came by and the driver sounded the horn. Joanda was out at the pump, getting a bucket of water. Mama and Lolly hurried out the front door. Mavis and Steve and Ricky jumped out of the back seat of the car. Daddy was plowing the field next to the house. When Joanda saw Miss Fenton and Miss Tyler in the front seat she turned to run.

"Don't go, Joanda," called Miss Fenton. "It's you I came to see. We are giving out garden seeds. Don't you want a couple of packets? What flowers do you like? Petunias? Nasturtiums? Prince's feather? Zinnias? Zinnias are so bright and pretty. They look nice in a bouquet to put on the table."

Joanda stood stiff like a stick of wood.

"How many do you want, Joanda?"

Joanda couldn't speak. No words would come.

"You'd have a pretty yard, if you'd clean it up and plant some flower beds," Miss Fenton went on. "Wouldn't you like to do that, Joanda?"

Mama, who was holding Lolly, came up closer to the car.

"This place don't belong to us, Miss Fenton," she said. "The boss-man and his wife wouldn't even thank us for it. They'd give us the dickens for doin' things like that."

Daddy came closer to the house with his tractor and its roaring drowned out the sound of voices. "Ricky! Come *here!*" Mama was terrified the boy would get in the way of the ma-

chine. "We don't want no more broken legs round here."

"You work for the Shands, don't you, Mrs. Hutley?" asked Miss Tyler.

"Yes ma'm," said Mama.

"They are friends of mine," said Miss Tyler. "I'm sure they'd be pleased if you took care of the place."

Miss Fenton looked at the tin cans, empty bottles, old rags and trash that littered the yard.

"Joanda, you're a big girl and you're not afraid of work. Why don't you rake up these tin cans and bottles and make your yard look nice?"

Still Joanda could not answer. She grasped the water bucket so tightly that her hand hurt.

"We've missed you at school, Joanda," Miss Fenton said gently.

"Next week on Friday, we're having Clean-Up Day," explained Miss Tyler. "The boys and girls are going to bring rakes and brooms and hoes and shovels. We're going to clean up the school yard so it looks as neat as a pin. We'll make flower beds and plant flower seeds. Won't you come and help us, Joanda?"

The girl shook her head. "Don't wanna come," she mumbled.

"We miss you very much, Joanda," repeated Miss Fenton. "Don't you want to pass to the next grade? If you are not sick, we will expect you back."

"It ain't hardly worth while now," spoke up Mama. "Cotton chopping time will soon be here."

"The cotton's just being planted, Mrs. Hutley," said Miss

Tyler. "The children won't be chopping until June. School lets out long before that."

"Here's a packet of zinnia seeds, Joanda," said Miss Fenton, "and one of carrots. You can plant a row at the edge of the cotton field. This packet has a verse on it."

Joanda did not reach out her hand.

Daddy's tractor came close again. It turned the corner, and roaring loudly, started off to the south. Joanda looked up to watch it. Then she saw Lolly out in the field behind it. The little girl was stumbling over the broken ground, calling to Daddy to give her a ride, but of course he could not hear her voice. She had on the new white shoes Daddy had bought her in town the previous Saturday.

Joanda flew. Her terror of the tractor was as great as her mother's. Daddy had come to a mud-puddle, pulled up and was about to back. He wanted to go through it fast so he wouldn't stick in it.

Joanda got there just before he backed. She took Lolly in her arms and held her tight. On her way to the house, she paddled her and told her not to go near the tractor. Lolly just laughed, but when she saw the mud on her new white shoes, she cried.

When Joanda got back, the teachers and the car were gone and Mama was in the kitchen. Joanda did not look at the seed packets until she had to set the table for supper. Then she picked them up and read the planting directions over.

"Want to hear the verse about carrots?" she asked.

"Sure do," said Mama.

Joanda read:

" 'Carrots are rich in Vitamin A,
  They'll make you strong for school or play;
  They'll keep your teeth without decay,
  And drive those horrid colds away.
  So plant these seeds some time in May,
  And you'll eat carrots every day.'

"I like that, Mama, don't you?" Joanda smiled as she hadn't smiled since the loss of the library book.

* * *

Some weeks later, on a Sunday, Uncle Shine appeared again. The Hutleys were eating dinner, when Trouble dashed out barking. There was the same old Ford and the same old man. The children clung to his hands and arms and pulled him in.

"We're not gonna let you go this time," said Ricky.

"We'll tie you to a tree and keep you here," said Joanda.

"I don't see any trees," laughed Uncle Shine, looking around.

"To a porch post then," said Steve.

"Jest in time for dinner, Uncle," called Mama. "You're invited this time."

All through dinner, the Hutleys talked about things that had happened to them since Christmas day. But Uncle Shine did not tell where he had been or what he had been doing. He just wanted to listen to Neva and her husband and children and to find out how they were getting along, he said. They took him out to see the cotton as soon as dinner was over.

"It's comin' up," cried Lolly. She ran into the field and tried to pull up a stalk but couldn't. Daddy laughed and said, "It sure is tough."

After the rains were over, the warm sun had come out and brought the cotton plants up, long rows of small green shoots, sprouting a few star-shaped leaves.

There was something hopeful about the sight. The annual ritual had begun again. Each year there was always new faith and hope that if the crop were good, the Hutleys—and thousands of other cotton farmers—could pay their debts and have a little left over. They did not ask for much—only the security of a bare living.

Daddy and Mama and Uncle Shine and the children stood at the edge of the field and they looked down the long rows.

"Looks like a good season this year," said Daddy. "Not too wet and not too dry."

"If only the army worms and the red spiders and leaf worms would go somewhere else," said Mama. "All that rain we had will sure bring bugs."

"We're lucky not to have the boll-weevil," said Daddy. "The weevil gits froze out up here in northern Arkansas, our winters are so cold. The poor devils that have to fight the boll-weevil can't never make a good crop. Jest look at this good black delta soil."

"When I was a young feller here," said Uncle Shine, "this was all woodland with virgin timber, and the lumber companies were just comin' in. The Mississippi River levee was always breakin' and causin' bad overflows. That's where your black soil came from—down that old river. When my Pa homesteaded up near the Missouri line, all his farm was under water except a ridge where he pastured his cows and horses. Long about 1914 when they began to grow the first cotton on new ground, it grew as high as a house, but was so weak it fell right over. Folks found out they had to grow corn for two or three years after clearin' the woodland, then plant cotton. Soil was too rich."

"They say this black soil won't never wear out," said Daddy. "Lucky for us. We don't pay a cent for fertilizer, 'cause we never put a drop on."

"Worst trouble we have is with grasshoppers," said Mama. "They come in July and eat the cotton flowers and all the leaves. They come in droves from them ditch-banks along the by-o."

"Soon as the old cotton goes to puttin' out leaves, we gotta go to choppin'," complained Mavis. "First time we chop, we gotta thin the plants in the row. Gotta chop it three times in all to git the weeds out."

"If we could jest be sure the price o' cotton would be good," said Daddy, "we'd work our heads off an' not mind it."

"Seems like a lot o' work for the little you get out of it," said Uncle Shine thoughtfully.

"I gotta make good this year," exclaimed Daddy, full of enthusiasm. "I wanta buy me some tools of my own. Big Charley's promised me the first tenant house that gits empty on his place."

"That's the way to talk!" said Uncle Shine. "Pull yourself up—there's no other way. Neva tells me you're a good carpenter. Is that so?"

"Oh, I do a little jack-leg carpenterin' when there's nothin' else to do," laughed Daddy, "jest between the jobs on the crop."

"I've bought me a little bungalow this side o' town," said Uncle Shine, "and I'm fixin' it over. I could use you in your spare time—day labor, you know."

"Oh, Uncle Shine! Are you gonna live there?" cried the children.

"Sure am," said the old man. "I'm tired of gallivantin'. I'm like the old horse—I've come home to roost, but not in a cotton field. I'd rather be near town."

The children clapped their hands. "And you'll come to see us every Sunday!"

"Maybe even during the week," laughed Uncle Shine.

It was Uncle Shine who suggested that Daddy start a bank account with the wages he paid him for his carpentry work. Uncle Shine kept on thinking of more and more jobs for him to do. He advised Daddy to get the full amount saved before making the purchase of the necessary tenant tools, so he would not have to pay more by buying in installments. Week by week Daddy's bank account began to grow.

One day Daddy came back from work, whistling gaily.

"What are you so tickled about, Daddy?" asked Joanda.

"Come and see what I brought, young un," answered Daddy.

The family crowded round as Daddy unloaded from the truck a white-painted door with a glass panel in it. He carried it up on the front porch.

"It's our'n!" he said with pride. "Uncle Shine bought his-self a newer fancier door, with an oval-shaped glass. He was goin' to throw this one out."

"Out! My goodness!" said Mama. "A good door with glass

in it! What you fixin' to do? This ain't *our* house, Dave. The Shands won't like it. . . ."

But Daddy already had the old door off its hinges and was fitting the new one in place. He told the boys to store the old door up in the loft, to be replaced if and when the Hutleys moved.

" 'Cause this is *our* door," he added, "and when we move we'll take it right along with us. I'll give it another coat of white paint. Then, wherever we live, people will know it's the Hutleys' house, when they see the pretty glass door!"

Mama brought warm water and a cloth and washed the glass window on both sides. It looked very beautiful. It let in *light*.

They all had to stand in the front room with the door shut to see how light it was.

Joanda looked at the newspaper-pasted walls. "If we could only have some pretty wallpaper . . ."

"And some new furniture," added Mama. "I keep thinking about that couch I picked out at Atkins' furniture store."

"And a couple of easy chairs to match," added Mavis.

"As if we ain't already got ten times too many places for our money," laughed Daddy.

They all went out in the road to see how the new door looked from the front.

"It makes the house look *all dressed up!*" cried Joanda.

"*All dressed up!*" echoed Lolly, clapping her hands.

Chadron State College Library
— Chadron, Nebraska

"Steve," said Mama, "go git the rake. Let's clean up some of this trash. Why don't we make a dump in one place back by the shed, and stop throwing trash around? Let's have Clean-Up day here like at school."

Joanda looked at Mama, her face beaming. "Can I make some flower-beds and plant those flower seeds? And a row of carrots at the edge of the cotton field?"

Mama put her arm around her. "You sure can, sugar."

CHAPTER VIII

On Wings of Fear

"Ricky, go to the house and pump your bucket full of water," said Joanda. "Hurry now, we're thirsty."

The small boy sat down in the row. "I don't want to," he said. "It's too heavy when it's full."

"Git it half full then," answered Joanda, "but you'll have to go twice as many times." She watched him as he started down the long cotton row, walking slowly toward the red shotgun house.

The cotton had grown quickly. The plants were six weeks old and nearly six inches tall, which meant it was time to chop. While Daddy plowed corn for Big Charley, all the family took their hoes and went out to the field which bordered on the bayou bank.

Big Charley had arranged for the four Burgess children to

chop, too. He also brought two truckloads of Negro choppers
of all ages out from town. They were working in a much
larger field joining Daddy's fifteen acres—a long row of workers moving steadily across the field.

Big Charley's straw-boss came over and showed the children
how he wanted the chopping done.

"Let two or three plants stand about twelve or sixteen inches
apart," he said. "Clean out all the weeds between. A good
cotton chopper stands straight and never bends over. He holds
his hoe like a broom, reaching over the row and hoeing toward
himself. Just walk along and keep hoeing as you go. Don't
leave any long skips."

Joanda and the children listened and tried to do just as the
man said. It was June now and the sun was hot. *Down, up,
down, up,* the children walked along the rows swinging their
hoes. The Burgess boys and Steve were soon far ahead. The
Burgess twins kept abreast of Mama, Joanda and Mavis. Lolly
played in the dirt.

Now and then a wave of made-up song from the Negro
workers in the big field was carried over the breeze: "*I's gwine
to town . . . I's gwine to town . . . I's gwine to buy me a new
hat and gown . . .*" Sometimes it was a hymn: "*Lord, I want
to be like Jesus . . .*"

"Ain't cotton the purtiest stuff you ever saw?" asked Joanda.
"I jest like to look at it. I think ours is the purtiest in the
county. It's growin' so fast, it's gittin' knee-high . . ."

"What's purty about cotton?" complained Mavis. "Before
it gits knee-high, we gotta chop it again. All we do is chop,
chop, chop!"

"*Chop, chop, chop,*" echoed Lolly. She was tired of her dirt pies now and began to throw dirt. She threw it over Mavis's head and in her eyes.

"Quit that, young un!" scolded Mavis. "You jest do that again and I'll set your clothes afire!"

"I'll take her back to the house," said Mama. "I don't feel good. I got to lie down awhile. Mavis, you tell the straw boss when he comes."

Mama and Lolly walked back to the house. After a long time Ricky returned with the water. He went to all the choppers one by one and they dipped up water in the dipper and drank. Then the bucket was empty again.

"I can't find our lunch, Nannie," said Ricky.

"Where'd you put it?" asked Joanda.

"Down in the shade at the end of the row," said Ricky.

"But I told you not to leave it in the grass," scolded Joanda, " 'cause it might could git antses all over it. Why didn't you put it in the boss's truck? Now I gotta stop work and go look for it."

Joanda and Ricky hunted through the tangled grass and weeds along the bayou bank. Soon they heard a dog growling.

"There's that old Trouble!" cried Joanda. "He's got our baloney and he's eatin' it."

"I'll whack him good!" Ricky chased the dog but could not catch him.

"That dog's always makin' trouble," said Joanda. "Ketchin' people's chickens, barkin' at cars, gittin' that salmon can stuck on his head, and now eatin' our baloney. Like Mama said, he sure was born for trouble, that's why she named him that."

"What are we gonna eat now?" asked Ricky.

"Go back to the house and git some more water," said Joanda. "Tell Mama, Trouble took our baloney. Maybe she'll give you something else for us to eat. Tell her we're powerful hungry."

The small boy trudged slowly across the field. Joanda wondered if she could wait until he made the long slow trip to the house and back again. She kept on chopping. Now she was far behind the others. *Down, up, down, up, down, up* . . . Her back began to hurt, so she straightened it. The trick was not to bend your back. She had heard Mama say that often and the straw boss said so, too. The weeds had started growing, and the stems of the cotton plants were strong and wiry.

It was hard to chop them off.

> *"Must Jesus bear the cross alone,*
> *And all the world go free . . ."*

She could hear the Negroes singing again. Their rich voices floated across the field. She rested her hoe to listen. She wished she could sing too, but chopping made her too tired.

Then she felt hungry again. Would Ricky never come? The others were all eating at the straw-boss's truck on the far side of the field. At last she heard Ricky calling and decided Mama wanted her to come to the house to eat. She dropped her hoe and ran to meet him.

"Mama wants you," said Ricky, panting. "She said tell Nannie . . . come quick . . . git Daddy . . ."

"Is Mama sick?" asked Joanda. "She was all right this morning." She wondered why Mama had left the field and where she could find Daddy.

She and Ricky ran to the house. She saw her the first thing. Mama was half-sitting, half-lying on the floor of the back porch, leaning against the wall of the building. She looked as if she had fallen there and could not get to her feet again. Her hoe lay on the steps. Lolly was making mud pies in the yard.

Mama tried to speak. "Git Daddy . . ." she gasped. "Gone blacksmith shop . . . have plow welded . . . Ricky . . . keep Lolly."

Daddy must have stopped on his way to the blacksmith shop to tell Mama where he was going.

Joanda was so frightened she could not think, but she knew she must act quickly. She told Ricky to hold Lolly so the little girl would not follow her. Then she ran down the road toward the corner. The blacksmith shop was at the garage next to Brownie's store. It was a mile from the Hutleys' house. It took a long time to get there.

As Joanda came up, she saw Daddy in his truck starting off. "Goin' to town to buy a new plow for Big Charley," he called. "Can't git the old one welded. What you doin' here? Why ain't you choppin', Nannie?"

"*Stop, stop! Wait!*" called Joanda frantically. "Mama's . . ."

Daddy stopped, picked her up and listened. "Sounds like a heart attack," he said. He turned around and drove quickly back to the house.

Mama was still leaning against the wall, gasping for breath. With Joanda's help, Daddy carried her into the house and laid her on a bed. Lolly was screaming, but Ricky held her tight.

"You'll have to go git a doctor, Nannie," said Daddy. "Mama's bad off, she can't git her breath. I don't dare leave her . . . Go back to the store, ask Brownie to git a doctor to come quick. Ask him to phone Brother Davis, too." Daddy put pillows under Mama's head and began to fan her. "She's smotherin' . . . go as fast as you can, sugar."

After Joanda left the house, Bug Burgess came up. "Hi there, Ricky, you ole water boy, where's our water?"

"That you, Bug?" called Daddy from inside. "Chase home and ask your mother to come fast as she can git here. My wife's dyin'."

"Gee, Mr. Hutley, I sure will." The boy dashed off.

The tears streamed down Joanda's face as she ran. She never knew how she managed to go that mile the second time, except that she flew on wings of fear. Her feet seemed never to touch the ground. Brownie took one look at her white face and put in the calls for her. He phoned Mrs. Shands too, and offered to go to town and bring Uncle Shine out.

Joanda wanted to hurry back but she couldn't. She was tired all over. Her feet were so heavy she could hardly lift them. When she was halfway home, Mavis came running across the field.

"You jest better git out here and chop cotton, Joanda Hutley!" she scolded. "The straw-boss was plumb put out when he saw you and Mama was both gone and he was two choppers short. I told him you went to bring us some water, 'cause I saw you runnin' off with Ricky. Where you been—down to the store buyin' yourself some candy? Where's our water? We're about to die. . . . We ain't had but one drink all day, and I got a terrible sideache. I always git the sideache . . ."

Joanda stood still and listened. She was too numb and tired and grief-stricken to reply. Fear clutched her heart again—maybe Mama had died. . . . She came to her senses, found her feet and ran to the house. Still scolding, Mavis went back to the field.

When Joanda got there, Aunt Lessie was in the room with Mama and soon the doctor came. He went into the house and closed the door. All the time that the doctor was there, Joanda sat on the back porch, saying rhymes to keep Lolly and Ricky quiet.

> *"Peter went a-fishin'*
> *Caught a little tadpole,*
> *Put it in the kitchen,*
> *Took it off his pole.*
> *Sang a little song,*
> *Not very long—*
> *Doodlum doodlum doo,*
> *Now it's all gone."*

"Say another one," begged the children. Joanda went on:

> *"What did the peacock*
> *Say to the crane?*
> *I wish by golly*
> *We'd git some rain.*
> *Creek's all muddy,*
> *Pond's all dry,*
> *Wasn't for the tadpoles*
> *Everybody'd die."*

Joanda danced Lolly up and down as she said this one:

> *"Oh, my little boy,*
> *Who made your britches?*
> *Mammy cut 'em out*
> *And Daddy sewed the stitches."*

Joanda always ended it with: "*Who* made your britches, Lolly?" and Lolly always answered, "*You* did, Nannie, you know you did."

After a while, Joanda heard a car and thought it must be Uncle Shine. But it was Brother Davis and Mrs. Shands. The doctor came out just then and spoke to them. The preacher went in, but Mrs. Shands stopped for a moment. "The doctor said he gave her a shot and she can breathe now," she told the girl. "Has she been bad off?"

Joanda nodded. "Yes ma'm."

"Now don't you worry, Nannie." Mrs. Shands put her arm around her. "We'll take care of your Mama," she said and hurried in.

It was after five that evening when Mavis came back from the field.

"You got it nice and easy," she said to Joanda. "Sittin' on the porch in the shade and holdin' the baby all day. Tightwad went all the way to *his* house to git us water."

"*Sh!*" Aunt Lessie came to the back door. "Don't make a sound or she'll git worse."

"What's the matter?" whispered Mavis.

"Mama's sick," said Joanda. "She like to died."

"Oh, Nannie!" Mavis fell into her sister's arms and it was Joanda who did the comforting.

Aunt Lessie and Mrs. Shands moved Mama's bed beside an open window so she could get fresh air. They sat up all that night with her. Toward morning they went home. Daddy didn't work the next day, but he sent the children to the field to chop as usual. The work must go on—cotton did not wait.

Joanda stayed home to take care of Ricky and Lolly. She kept wishing Uncle Shine would come, but he didn't. In the middle of the morning, Mama had another heart attack.

"Nannie," called Daddy. "You'll have to go phone that doctor again. Brother Davis too."

Joanda's face turned white, as fear shook her. This time Mama would die. Lolly cried and screamed for Nannie to pick her up, but Joanda turned a deaf ear. For the first time she realized how selfish and demanding the baby—no longer a baby, but a big girl of three—had become. Had her own devotion made her so? All the way down the road she heard Lolly screaming, and she hoped Ricky could quiet her.

A car came suddenly up from behind. In it were Jed and Maggie Sutton who lived seven miles farther out the road. They stopped and Joanda explained her errand. They said they would telephone the preacher and the doctor, so Joanda turned back.

It was sad to look at Mama, so white and worn, struggling so hard for breath. At last the doctor came, and after he gave her the shot, she felt better. The doctor stayed most of the day and came back that night. The women returned and did what they could to help. Brother Davis came and prayed.

On the third day, Uncle Shine came, and Joanda felt easier. He had been away and just found the note that Brownie had left under his door.

The first words Mama spoke were to Uncle Shine. "The Lord sure can whoop us when He gits at it," she said. "I don't know what I done to deserve this. I'll have to try to lead a better life . . ."

On the fourth morning Mama wanted to get up, but Daddy and Uncle Shine wouldn't let her. The women went home and Uncle Shine stayed to help so Daddy could go back to his plowing.

The doctor's advice was not cheerful. He said that if Mama had another heart attack she must be taken to the hospital. And he said Mama must not chop any more cotton.

"But how will the cotton git chopped?" asked Mama.

*　　*　　*

It was Big Charley, the boss-man, who came to the rescue. He brought twenty geese, and Daddy built a run for them along the side of the shotgun house. They were to be turned into those cotton fields that were fenced to eat weeds and Johnson grass, so the cotton would not have to be chopped. It was fun to watch them. Each goose took a row and worked all day long eating the grass. They went to their trough to get water to drink, then went back to eat grass again.

The first time the children drove them to the field, Trouble barked and scattered them. It took a long time to get them in at the gate.

That night the children had to bring them back. Ricky went

ahead to keep them on the turn-row. Joanda came behind, stick in hand.

"Hurry up!" yelled Ricky. "You're too slow."

"If I go fast, they git tired and sit right down and rest," said Joanda. "Then I have to pick 'em up and carry 'em."

"Ugh!" said Ricky. "I wouldn't. I'd be a-scared they'd bite me." He began teasing a big fat goose and soon she was chasing him. "Stop her, Nannie! Stop her! She'll beat me to death with them big old wings. Don't let her bite me."

Joanda came to the rescue with her stick and soon had the flock in order again.

"If any geese ever chase *me*," she said when they reached the iron pump, "I'm not gonna pump 'em a drop of water."

Daddy came up. "Then they'll die," he said, "and you'll have to chop twenty big acres of cotton."

"Oh, I'll pump! I'll pump!" cried Joanda.

Soon the children were calling the pump "the goose pump," because the geese drank so much water. Every evening Joanda and Ricky pumped enough "goose water" to fill the large trough Daddy had made for them. The geese lined up on both sides of it, and lifting their heads high after each sip, drank and drank.

"They drink it as fast as we pump it," cried Joanda. Ricky got mad and splashed water all over them, but it only ran off their backs.

One time the geese got loose and ran straight to the bayou and had a swim. The children had to chase them back.

"Mama, I wish I was a goose," said Joanda. "I'd like to swim in the by-o, it's so nice and cool down there."

"You'd change your mind if I got after you with a gun," said Mama. She was sitting up by the window every day now.

Joanda looked at her mother in surprise. "Are you fixin' to shoot the boss-man's geese?"

"Yes," laughed Mama, "if they don't hush their quackin' and stop gittin' so much dust in here. When they're in the pen, they keep runnin' up and down the fence all day long. They make more dust than a car on a dirt road, and it all comes in here. If I close the windows, I'll smother sure."

"Seems like geese just try theirself to make people mad," said Joanda thoughtfully.

"If they run by my window one more time, I'll shoot 'em every one!" declared Mama.

"Better wait till you can aim a little better, Neva," laughed Daddy.

[115]

"They pester us more than they help," said Mama.

"They don't do any sech of a thing," said Joanda stoutly. "If Daddy gits shet of the geese, he won't have *me* to chop the old cotton."

And so the Hutleys put up with the geese.

The children made up a game they called "geesy feathers." The yard was filled with feathers now. Joanda tied two or three of them on the end of a string. Lolly ran and pulled it, the feathers flying in the air above her. Ricky and Steve stuck feathers in the soft ends of corncobs, pitched them up in the air and sailed them. The goose feathers were fun, and because of the geese, the children went back to school again.

The summer session at the split-term school opened on July 15th, to run to the end of August. Joanda's sorrow over the lost library book was now a thing of the past. She was eager to go to school again. It was hot in the schoolhouse in midsummer, but not as hot as out in the cotton field.

It was good to be back. There were three shelves full of good library books to read; there was the pretty lunch room, and there was Miss Fenton. Joanda was glad it was not a new teacher. She had so much to tell her.

"I brought you some zinnias, the last ones," she said shyly, handing out a small bouquet. "I put two old tires around the flower-beds to keep Trouble off, but the mean ole geese trampled 'em down."

"Geese?" asked Miss Fenton.

"After Mama's two heart attacks, she couldn't chop cotton any more," Joanda explained. "I couldn't either, and we got way behind. So the boss-man brought geese to eat the Johnson grass. The doctor says Mama has to have all her teeth pulled. She's got malaria too . . ."

"I'm sorry," said Miss Fenton.

"That library book . . . the one I took home . . ." Joanda dropped her eyes. It was hard to go on, but she knew she must. "I dropped it in a mud-puddle and messed it up . . . so I jest threw it in the by-o . . . That's why I couldn't come back to school."

It was out now, and she felt better.

"But now you are back, and I'm glad."

Miss Fenton put a comforting arm around her.

CHAPTER IX

Lamp in the Window

"Sun up in the mornin'
Hot upon my back,
Got to go start pickin'
Cotton in my sack . . .

Hot old sun keeps shinin'
Heavy grows my pack,
Pick, pick, pick, keep pickin'
Cotton in my sack . . ."

Where had the summer gone to? Joanda was picking cotton again, singing her little cotton song.

By midsummer the cotton buds had come out, creamy colored, pink, then red. They started blooming at the bottom of the big shiny-leaved plants, so were scarcely noticed.

The "squares" formed first, each square developing into a bloom. On the third day after the bloom opened, it withered and fell off, leaving a tiny boll on the stalk.

The sun shone hotter and hotter and baked the earth hard beneath. As the lovely cotton flowers faded, the hard green bolls grew larger. Then the bolls began to burst, exposing mounds of fluffy white cotton.

Now it was October again—cotton picking time. School was out and "cotton vacation" had begun. The cotton country came to life, with renewed activity in the fields, at the gins and at the stores in town. Again the same old ritual was followed by everybody—work from "can see" to "can't see," get weighed up and paid off, and on Saturday go to town to spend.

On the first trip they made to town that fall, Mama and Joanda and Lolly and Ricky went to see Uncle Shine in his little house. They admired it from top to bottom, then sat down to visit.

"How's the cotton makin', Neva?" asked Uncle Shine.

"Sorry crop as usual," said Mama. "If I could jest pick, I wouldn't feel so bad about it. Seems like it'll kill me to set at home all day long, when I know the others are all out in the field."

"Time you looked after yourself," said Uncle Shine. "How you doin'?"

"I'm feelin' hearty again, thanks to you, Uncle," said Mama. "If you hadn't offered to pay my doctor bills, I think I'd a died in one of them spells. I wouldn't a had the heart to go on."

"If Dave is banking his crop money, he'll soon have enough for that farm machinery he wanted to get," said Uncle Shine. "What is it he wants?"

"A breakin' plow and cultivator first," said Mama. "Then a section harrow and planter, a wagon or trailer and some hoes. It'll take about $300 all together—he ain't saved that. Then there's the mules—that'll be another $300—if we're to be tenants next year. Why, it'll take us three or four years . . ."

"Hum!" said Uncle Shine, thinking hard.

"When cotton pickin' started, Dave was $204 in debt to Big Charley for our 'furnish' since March," said Mama. "His half of the first three bales paid that off. He gits half, but all the pickin' comes out of his half. If he'd only save the rest of the crop money . . . But he's never saved. He don't know how."

"We might could help him," said Uncle Shine.

"I don't know," said Mama sadly. "If he'd store some of the cotton for a higher price . . . But he rushes each load to the gin and sells it, and first thing I know the money's gone. He bought a bicycle for Steve and a tricycle for Ricky and every Saturday he has to have a good time. If the boss-man would jest make him store some of the cotton—but I reckon Big Charley wants quick money, too."

"I'll see Big Charley," said Uncle Shine.

"What do you mean?" asked Mama.

"How much is a load of cotton worth?" asked Uncle Shine.

"Jest now, the boss-man gits about $190 a load," said Mama. "Dave gits half o' that, less the pickin', but it goes quick. One trip to town and his pockets are empty. I don't know what he does with it."

"He's not puttin' it in the bank?"

"Not that I know of," said Mama. "I'm worried—he's spendin' so much. We can live on our cotton-pickin' money and we could put our crop-money by. Come January and

February we'll be needin' it. Them's the hard months—bad weather and no work and the family still eats. But this spendin', it's part of the cotton farmer's life. It's in our blood. I can't never hardly save a penny myself. We do without all year, then when we git some money, we try to buy . . . happiness . . . with it, but it slips through our fingers."

"Uncle Shine, I'm gonna save every penny I git for pickin' cotton this year," spoke up Joanda.

"Huh!" said Ricky. "You're talkin' big."

Uncle Shine smiled and turned to Mama. "We must help Dave pay for those mules," he said. "Can you . . ?" He stopped, glancing at Joanda and Ricky. "You take Lolly outside and wait in my car, Nannie."

"But what . . ?" said Joanda, full of curiosity.

Mama and Uncle Shine talked for a long time, then Uncle Shine drove them to the Goodwill, where they waited for Daddy to come. The store was crowded with many people, Mexicans, Negroes and whites. Soon a storm came up and more people rushed in off the sidewalk to get out of the rain.

Maggie Sutton and Lessie Burgess came over to talk to Mama.

"How you doin'?" asked Mama.

"I'm hot and bothered," said Aunt Lessie, fanning.

"I'm fair to middlin'," said Maggie Sutton. "I'm sure glad to see you better, Neva. That was a close shave you had in the summer."

"Yes," said Mama. "Guess the Lord has work for me to do —that's why He didn't take me. But it ain't pickin' cotton, for the doctor won't let me."

"Time you taken a little rest," said Aunt Lessie. "They've

brought in so many Mexicans to pick this year, it's a wonder there's cotton enough to go around. Gentle Annie! It's gonna rain sure as the world!"

"That storm last night give me the wide-awakes," said Maggie Sutton.

The rain came pouring down. It began to thunder, and lightning flashed. Suddenly the electric lights all over the store went out. Joanda clung to Mama, frightened for the moment.

Aunt Lessie looked around on all sides, her round face beaming in the semi-darkness. "We're all the same color when the lights are out," she said softly.

"Ain't it the truth!" said Maggie Sutton.

"Reckon it don't matter a mite to the Lord what color our skin is," said Mama.

Joanda felt better and everybody smiled as the lights flashed on again.

"Lordy mercy! Look at it pour," said Aunt Lessie. "Pity the poor folks too lazy to bring their cotton in under cover. My Pa always said the rain's God's fertilizer. It comes down on rich and poor alike."

"Mama, is it gonna keep on rainin' and spoil our crop?" asked Joanda.

"No, sugar," said Mama.

"Sun'll be so hot tomorrow," said Aunt Lessie, "we'll be wishin' for a good shower like this to cool us off."

Aunt Lessie was right. Saturday's rain was soaked up by the dry earth like a thirsty sponge. By Monday, no signs of it remained. At six in the morning, the sun was hot and bright.

"Dew's off," said Daddy to the children. "Take your pick sacks and go to the patch."

The day was unusually hot. Joanda and Jolene Burgess picked along parallel rows, dragging their long pick sacks behind them. A crowd of some fifty Negro pickers were at work in the next field. Joanda heard them singing:

> " 'Oh, Lordy,
>   Pick a bale o' cotton,
>   Oh, Lordy,
>   Pick a bale a day.
>
> Gonna jump down turn around
> Pick a bale o' cotton;
> Gonna jump down turn around
> Pick a bale a day.

Me and my wife can
Pick a bale o' cotton;
Me and my wife can
Pick a bale a day.

Pick-a, pick-a, pick-a, pick-a
Pick a bale o' cotton;
Pick-a, pick-a, pick-a,
Pick a bale a day.

Oh, Lordy,
Pick a bale o' cotton,
Oh, Lordy,
Pick a bale a day.' "

Tiny Joe Healy, a little Negro boy, came over and asked, "Where's Tightwad and Steve? I got a riddle to tell 'em. 'Crooked as a cat, teeth like a tree . . .' "

"Don't you go to pickin' on my row, Tiny Joe," said Joanda. "You go pick by your mammy."

"I's gonna pick the end pieces for Tightwad and Steve," said the boy. "Where's they at?"

"Over that-a-way," said Joanda nodding.

By mid-afternoon, Joanda and Jolene were hot, tired and listless. Suddenly a hard green cotton boll landed at Joanda's feet. Both girls came to sudden life.

"Those boys!" exclaimed Joanda. "They want another cotton boll fight."

The girls looked up but saw no one.

"They're duckin'," said Jolene. "They're afraid your Daddy will see 'em."

"I hear the stalks rustlin'," said Joanda. "They're comin' close. Let's git our ammunition ready."

Hastily the girls picked off as many bolls as they could. But still they hadn't located the boys, although an occasional boll landed near them.

"Bet they're after our watermelons," said Joanda. "Daddy'll tan their hides good if they steal his ripe ones."

"That's jest where they've been," said Jolene. "I see Tightwad's red cap down in that lower part of the field. Now they're comin' this way. Now they're startin' . . . ."

A volley of bolls showered the girls. Mavis and Arlene came creeping back down their rows to help win the battle. The four girls threw bolls as fast as they could pick them up.

"Golly, I got hit!" cried Joanda. "Ouch! Stop, you boys. You hit me in the eye."

"Don't yell," scolded Mavis. "You want Daddy to come? Can't we have a little fun once instead of workin' all the time?"

Joanda quieted down and the battle of the bolls continued. Back and forth went the hard weapons, accompanied by loud snickers and guffaws. The boys seemed to have unlimited ammunition.

"Stop!" cried Jolene. "I got hit, too."

"Two casualties," cried Steve from the other side. "Let's knock out the other two."

"Boys!" shrieked Mavis. "There comes Daddy. You better scoot!"

The boys took to their heels, but Dave Hutley was already after them. "Bring back my watermelons," he called. "The ripest melons are gone from my patch."

[125]

As the boys ran across the road, a large watermelon fell to the ground and broke into pieces. Tiny Joe Healy grabbed up the pieces and ran off eating. The other boys came back and Daddy saw they had no watermelons on them. He sent them back to their pick sacks. "Quit chuckin' cotton bolls," he ordered. "We won't have any cotton if you chuck 'em all off."

"Betcha Tiny Joe will cry hisself to sleep with the stomach ache tonight," said Joanda, laughing.

When weighing-up time came, the boys seemed to have extra heavy sacks. "How'd you boys git so much cotton picked, wastin' all that time fightin'?" asked Daddy. "This sack sure weighs heavy—ten pounds heavier than usual."

The boys' faces turned red and they winked at each other, as Daddy wrote down the heavy weights in his cotton record book.

"Won't you pay us off before we empty our sacks, Mr. Hutley?" asked Bug Burgess.

"No sir, I only pay after I see what kind of cotton's been picked," said Daddy with a twinkle in his eye.

J. T. Burgess came into the field and watched.

Bug climbed up on the trailer, with Steve behind him. Then Tightwad climbed up. All three boys emptied their sacks. First came out white snowy cotton, then some heavy green objects.

"New kind of green cotton you been growin', Dave, I see!" said J. T.

"Extra heavy kind too!" laughed Daddy.

The boys had the weight of the watermelons taken off their records and then they were paid off. Daddy took the money out of a cigar box full of change that he brought with him. Daddy decided that since the melons were picked, they might as well be eaten. He sent them down to the bayou for cooling. Later, Mama and Lolly and Ricky came to the field, and they all went over to the bayou bank and had a watermelon picnic.

"I must go git my truck and haul that cotton to town," said Daddy.

"Let it go till morning," said Mama. "It's late now and I've got supper ready."

"Don't like to leave it out in the field," said Daddy.

"It'll be all right so near your house," said J. T. "Got a tarpolian to cover it?"

"Yes," said Daddy. "I'll go git it."

The children threw their pick sacks over their shoulders and walked home. Down the highway ran trucks full of cotton-pickers, laughing and talking, being carried back to town after a day of picking.

Joanda and Jolene followed the footpath along the bayou.

"Who's that?" said Joanda suddenly.

Jolene looked. A shabby old man, dressed in a loose-fitting coat, was scurrying along the path in front of them.

"It looks like Uncle Shine," said Joanda. "*Uncle Shine! Uncle Shine!*"

But the man did not stop or answer the girl's calls. He walked fast and soon disappeared.

"It looked like Uncle Shine, didn't it?"

"Yes," said Jolene. "Maybe he's twins, though, and it was the other one."

"He's not a twin," said Joanda. "His only brother was Mama's daddy. He died when he was a young man. I heard Mama say so."

When Joanda reached home, Mama had supper ready and they all sat down and ate. Darkness fell and the light of the lamp threw a glow on the faces round the table, making the scene one of peace and beauty. But soon the quiet was shattered—the geese set up a noisy honking.

"Them geese will drive me out of my mind!" exclaimed Mama. "I wish the boss-man would take 'em back again. We don't need 'em any more."

Daddy jumped to his feet. "They're better than watch-dogs," he said. "They always make a noise when they're scared—when there's something around to scare them."

"Why, what could there be to scare 'em?" laughed Mama.

"There's nothin' scary with all the cotton growin' all around everywhere . . ."

Daddy went out and looked, then came in again.

"Did you see anything?" asked Mama.

"Only old Trouble sittin' on his tail," he said. "Let's go to bed. I'm dog-tard."

It was in the middle of the night when the geese honked again.

"I tell you somebody's prowlin' around here and not for any good." Daddy sprang out of his bed and took his shotgun off the wall.

"Who do you think you're gonna shoot, Dave?" asked Mama quietly.

"Any thief that tries to take my cotton," said Daddy. "I don't care who he is." He hurried out the back door.

Mama lighted the lamp quickly and set it on the window sill on the west side of the house.

"If there's a chicken thief around," she said to the frightened children who crowded close, "this light will scare him off quick and git him to runnin'. Then Daddy won't shoot him. Chicken stealin' is wicked, but I don't believe a body should be *killed* for stealin' a chicken. Maybe they're not wicked, but jest hungry."

Joanda stared at Mama, wide-eyed.

"But, Mama," she managed to say, "we ain't got no chickens."

When Daddy came back, he still had seen no one and had found nothing wrong. He went to bed and when the geese honked the third time, he was too tired and sleepy to go.

The next morning, he hurried out to the cotton field and soon returned. "Our cotton's stole—that whole trailerful!" he announced.

"Oh, it can't be," said Mama. "Nobody would take it."

"Did you hear them geese again as I was goin' to sleep?" asked Daddy. "Why didn't you make me go out?"

"Because I thought nobody was there and because I thought the cotton was safe," said Mama.

Daddy sat down and covered his face with his hands. The old feeling of discouragement and hopelessness came over him.

"It had to be mine," he said, "the only trailer of cotton in this whole big county that gits stole. What will Big Charley say—after he's helped and trusted me so much?"

"I heard of three other loads bein' stole right near here," said Mama.

"How can I ever git ahead?" Daddy went on. "There's always somethin' to hold a sharecropper back. Your children break their legs, your wife gits heart attacks, your cotton gits stole. What's the use o' tryin' any more?"

"But them things can happen to *any*body, Dave," said Mama.

Steve came bursting in: "I saw footsteps made by great big shoes. They're all around the trailer. The rustler must have toted it off in pick sacks. Golly! This is wonderful, jest like in the movin' pitchers. To think of it happenin' to *us!* Can't I go call the sheriff?"

"The scales are gone and all the pick sacks," cried Ricky. "That mean ole cotton rustler musta took 'em with him."

"Listen to them kids!" said Daddy. "Talkin' about footprints and cotton rustlers and sheriffs. You boys listen to me—don't you say nary a word about this to nobody or I'll tan your hides so you can't sit down. Run over to Big Charley's and tell him to come here right away."

The boys left and Daddy just sat there, studying over his bad fortune. "It's all your fault, Neva," he said angrily. "*You* told me to leave that cotton out in the field over night. *You* set a lamp in the window to warn that fella I was comin' out after him. Did you *want* that rustler to steal our cotton?"

"Yes," said Mama. "I'd rather have *him* steal the cotton than have *you* shoot him."

CHAPTER X

Take It and Welcome

"I hear you had some cotton stole," said Brownie, the store-keeper, getting out of his car.

"Bad news travels fast," said Dave Hutley.

Other cars drove up.

Big Charley and his wife came at once when they heard the news. Maggie and Jed Sutton dropped in. Uncle Shine came out from town. All the people stood in the yard talking. The children gawked and listened.

"Did you git the law on 'em?" asked Brownie.

"I called the police," said Big Charley. "They said they'd go to all the gins and try to locate it."

"How did it happen, Dave?" asked Brownie.

Dave Hutley told the whole story.

"The police will never find it," said Brownie. "It's been

took by some one right around here and put with their own cotton. Only some one who handles cotton would do it."

"That's right," said Big Charley. "No stranger could sell cotton at any of the gins. The gins only buy cotton from people they know."

"Probably some one with a truck saw it and put it in their truck and went on and had it baled with their cotton at the gin," said Brownie. "They needed your cotton, Dave, to make out an even bale."

The men laughed.

"The pick sacks are gone too," said Dave. "Maybe we can trace *them*."

"And the scales," added Steve.

"One thing's sure. They had a shotgun with 'em," said Big Charley. "I could see prints of it down on the ground where they leaned it up against the truck. They made sure of being safe."

"There's a new family of sharecroppers just moved into one of Burgess's houses," said Brownie.

"But J. T. wouldn't put crooks in any of his croppers' houses," said Mama.

"You can't tell what you're gittin' in sharecroppers these days," said Brownie. "There's all kinds."

"The first thing any man would do," said Mrs. Shands, "he'd look see who lives around him."

"But how would I feel to accuse some one unjustly?" asked Dave.

"We could at least look for the pick sacks and scales," said Big Charley.

"Where'll we go?" asked Dave.

"Let's go see those new croppers of Burgess's first," said Jed Sutton. "Has J. T. been over?"

"No," said Dave. "He hasn't come."

"That looks funny," said Brownie. "J. T. sure totes a good name, but . . ."

"Listen here, Brownie," said Mama hotly, "I won't have nobody accusing J. T. J. T. never stole no cotton and you know it well as I do."

"Those new croppers wouldn't have a truck of their own," broke in Uncle Shine. "If they stole the cotton, how could they dispose of it?"

"They'd use J. T.'s truck," said Brownie.

"J. T.'s an honest man," declared Mama.

"Let's go see," said Big Charley. "Maybe them new croppers . . ."

"J. T. won't like this," said Dave.

"He won't find out about it," said Jed Sutton.

"I'll go with you," said Uncle Shine.

The men got into Big Charley's car in silence and drove off up the road. It wasn't long till they were back again.

"Find anything?" asked Mama.

"Place is bare as a bone," said Dave.

"Only a couple sticks o' furniture," said Big Charley.

"No place to hide cotton except a damp storm cellar and it was full of tin cans and snakes," growled Uncle Shine.

"The folks home?" asked Mama.

"No—all out in J. T.'s south field, pickin'," said Dave. "We jest looked around without askin'." He sat down in a chair, dejected. "I don't like this snoopin'. I won't go around accusin' my neighbors."

"But them croppers are new—they're not neighbors!" said Jed Sutton.

"They've come here to work and live," said Dave. "We'd ought to treat 'em like neighbors. Look what you folks done for me when I was new in the neighborhood and needed help. Look how you paid off that doctor bill for Ricky's leg. I ain't never forgot that, and never will. If any o' my neighbors took my cotton, I won't go spyin' on 'em. I say—take it and welcome."

"I say so too," said Uncle Shine. "How 'bout you, Neva?"

"We sure do need the money . . ." said Neva, "but Dave's right. Take it and welcome."

"You're too soft, Hutley," said Jed Sutton. "That family's *new* . . ."

"I'll be soft then," said Dave. "I know how it feels to be a new sharecropper in a strange place. No cropper would start out by stealin' cotton. And if my other neighbors need my cotton bad enough to steal it, they can have it for what they did for me."

"I know how you feel," said Brownie, scratching his head. "I'd feel the same. But there's more and more o' this rustlin' goin' on right under our noses. How's it gonna be stopped?"

"Isn't there something you can *do?*" cried Mrs. Shands impatiently. "Are all you men just going to let the thief have it?"

"If it was me," said Jed Sutton, "I'd leave another load out in the field, hide with a shotgun, pick 'em off and *see* who done it!"

"No," said Big Charley. "I feel like Dave does. We've both got to take the loss."

Dave nodded.

"Be sure to bring all your cotton back to the house every night after this, Dave," Big Charley went on, "if you can't get it to the gin. Pile it on your front porch, or tie your dog to the wagon wheel."

"I sure will," said Dave. "It was all my fault. The geese warned us, but . . ."

The men turned to go.

Mrs. Shands spoke to Mama. "Look at these men, throwing our money away. I needed that hundred dollars . . . but no worse than you needed yours."

Mama said, "Bad luck seems bound to come, no matter how hard we try."

After the excitement, the children had to go back to picking again. Despite interruptions, cotton picking went on—each day the same hot sun, the endless long rows, the tiresome back bending. Big Charley brought over old pick sacks to pick in and Uncle Shine stayed out to help. He had not picked since he was eighteen years old, so he had to learn all over again.

One morning soon after the cotton theft, Joanda was the first one to reach the field. As she came up to the empty trailer, Trouble jumped out and barked. Joanda stared. There were the lost pick sacks hanging over the tail-board.

She picked them up one by one. There was Mavis's long nine-foot sack—it had cost two dollars new; and Steve's old one with the patches on it; her own seven-footer with the hole she had never had time to mend; Ricky's short little tow sack;

and Lolly's sugar sack. They all looked as usual.

Joanda stood still, wondering how they came there. Trouble kept on barking. Then she saw Uncle Shine's coat. It was hanging on the wooden arm at the back of the trailer where the scales used to hang before they were stolen. Uncle Shine must have forgotten to take his coat home the night before.

Still thinking about the pick sacks, Joanda took the coat down. Uncle Shine would be back to pick again today, but he never came till late. The coat had something heavy in the pocket. Joanda put her hand in and pulled out . . . Big Charley's weighing scales.

She stared at them—then dropped them like a hot potato. What did this mean? Joanda was stunned.

The thief had returned. He had brought the pick sacks

back. He had brought the scales back and put them in Uncle Shine's pocket. He must have been afraid to keep such direct evidence for fear of some identification on them. He had been afraid to throw the scales away for fear his act would be traced, so the only thing he could do was to bring them back. He had brought them back and put them in Uncle Shine's coat pocket, to make it look as if Uncle Shine were the thief.

Joanda stared at the scales on the ground. What should she do with them? Should she put them back in Uncle Shine's pocket and let him be caught?

Then all at once she knew that Uncle Shine was the thief. But her feeling of loyalty was so great, she knew she must protect him. She would not put the scales in his pocket. She laid them on top of the pile of pick sacks, and went down the row to start her picking.

She hadn't long to wait. Steve came out with the water bucket, discovered the scales and pick sacks and went tearing back to the house to tell Daddy.

Big Charley brought a truckload of pickers out from town. All that day as she picked, Joanda was sick at heart. She couldn't forget that shabby old man's figure she had seen on the bayou path the evening before the cotton was stolen. It seemed incredible that Uncle Shine was a thief and had stolen her own Daddy's cotton, but she knew it was true.

Everybody was excited over the news of the return of the scales and the sacks, but it did not help in the solution of the theft. Nobody connected it with Uncle Shine, and Joanda was glad she had found the scales and taken them out of his coat.

The cotton picking went on. Lolly came to the field with Joanda every day now, since she had learned to play quietly and did not bother the pickers. Today she gathered dry cotton bolls and filled her pocket with them. "I got a bunch o' money in my pocket," she said, patting it.

"That's nice, sugar," said Joanda, "what you gonna buy?"

"New coat, new hat, new shoes," said Lolly. "I'm goin' up yonder to my house."

"Stay here with me, Lolly. Mama's layin' down and takin' a nap," said Joanda. "Nobody to talk to you there."

"I mean to *my* house," said the little girl. In a nest of morning glory vines she had hollowed out holes for play-bedroom and kitchen.

"What you got there, sugar?" asked Joanda.

"I found me a little birdie, it's gonna live with me in my house." Lolly had a dove with a hurt wing in her hand.

"See you don't hurt the poor thing," said Joanda. "Git your bonnet on, sugar, or you'll git your nose a-burnin'."

"It's too hot, I threw it off," said Lolly. She ran to Joanda. "I want me a nickel," she said.

"Wait till this evenin' when we go to the store," said Joanda.

Lolly ran to the trailer and began to swing on the axle under it, in the shade. Then she came running to Joanda. She had a fuzzy caterpillar on her sleeve. "Git that old worm off me. I'm a-scared of them kind."

Joanda brushed it off. "Now, go play with your birdie, sugar, and let Nannie pick. Nannie's gonna git her sack *plumb full* today."

"I wanna stay with you, Nannie," said Lolly.

[139]

"If I tell you about the rabbit, will you go to your play-house and play?" asked Joanda.

Lolly clapped her hands and nodded yes, so Joanda recited:

" 'The rabbit skip,
The rabbit hop,
The rabbit bit
My turnip top.
Ho ho, rabbit, ho ho!

That rabbit run,
That rabbit flew,
That rabbit tore
His shirt in two.
Ho ho, rabbit, ho ho!' "

" 'Ho ho, rabbit, ho ho!' " sing-songed Lolly as she went back to her nest of vines.

Joanda picked busily, her two hands never stopping. Mavis and Steve were far ahead in their rows and she wanted to catch up. She saw that Uncle Shine had come and Ricky was with him. She must pick fast—she couldn't talk to Uncle Shine today, now that she knew he was a thief. He and Ricky were talking. As they came closer, she listened.

"Mama was the best picker of us all," said Ricky. "Daddy teased her and said the cotton just jumped out of the bolls into her sack."

"Wish it would start jumpin' into my sack," said Uncle Shine. "I'm 'fraid I'll give out before nighttime comes."

Joanda watched Ricky picking in the next row. "I see why you're comin' so fast, Ricky, you're jest goose-pickin' it. You got to git all the cotton out of the boll with one pull. Dig down in with your fingers and tear it loose."

"I can't git it out," said Ricky.

"I can't either," said Uncle Shine.

"I wish I was some place where I'd never see any cotton to pick," said Ricky.

"Me, too," said Uncle Shine.

"*Or to steal*, I s'pose," added Joanda under her breath, glancing up at Uncle Shine.

"I don't mind pickin' cotton when it's cool," came Mavis's voice from up front, "but the trouble is, it gits hot."

"Oh, does it!" cried Steve.

Joanda looked ahead. "Oh, you old Steve, git off my row. This is *my* row."

"Yes," said Steve. "You take the best row with all the big bolls on it."

"I'm pickin' where Daddy told me to pick," said Joanda.

"It's easier where it's real short, in a sand-blow," called Jolene Burgess off to one side. "The stalks don't hit you in the face all the time."

"I'll go git me a new row all my own," said Joanda, moving to another part of the field. "You kids better finish out your rows and not leave any skips."

Now she was away from Uncle Shine and would not have to talk to him. Hearing Lolly's voice, she did not bother to look back. Her new row was good, and her two hands fluttered like bees from one boll to the next, while her right kept moving backwards, pushing big bunches of cotton into her sack. She was so busy she forgot about Lolly. She had only

one thought—*Uncle Shine is a thief, Uncle Shine is a thief* . . .
Suddenly she remembered she hadn't heard the little girl's
voice for a long time.

"*Lolly!*" she called, but no answer came.

Joanda hated to stop her work when her sack was so nearly
full. She stood up and stretched. Then she threw off her sack
and walked back to Lolly's little vine house. Lolly was not
there. She was not under the trailer playing in the shade or
swinging on the axle. She was not up on the bed of cotton inside the trailer.

"*Lolly! Lolly! Where are you?*" called Joanda. She
climbed up on the trailer ladder and looked across the field.
She couldn't see a little pink sunbonnet anywhere.

"Steve, have you seen Lolly?" she called.

Joanda called Mavis and Rickey and Uncle Shine and the

other pickers, but none of them had seen Lolly. She raced up and down the cotton rows, hunting and calling, stopping to look under the bushes. In the unpicked rows, the bushes were so large they touched in the middles. But Lolly could not be found.

The other pickers were too busy, they did not offer to help. Every minute meant more money in their pockets that night. They couldn't stop picking.

"Oh, she'll turn up," said one of the women from town. "My young uns was always gittin' lost in the cotton when they was little. But they always turned up again."

"You'd better git to pickin', Nannie," scolded Mavis. "Daddy'll beat you over the head if you don't git your sack full."

"He won't do any such of a thing and you know it," retorted Joanda. "But Lolly—*where's Lolly?* I can't find her anywhere . . ."

"You won't make a dollar today if you don't keep at your pickin'," said Steve.

"*What do I want with a dollar when Lolly's lost?*" cried Joanda.

Up and down the rows she went, hunting and calling. There were acres and acres of cotton on all sides as far as the eye could see, one great field after another. It was all high— so high it concealed the curly red head of a little girl walking in the middles.

Joanda stopped to think. Surely she could see the stalks wiggling and that would tell her somebody was there. But no. A wind had come up and was moving the cotton branches, now here, now there. She couldn't run everywhere. It was hopeless. Then she thought of the bayou and her heart sank. *What if Lolly fell in the by-o and got drowned?*

The thought was too horrible. She pushed the panic out of her mind and tried to reason calmly. *It's dusky-dark already . . .* she thought, *soon it will be night . . . I can't go home without her . . . she can't sleep out all night . . .*

On her way to the stream, she saw that the town pickers had quit work and were weighing up. They were helping to look too. All over the field, people were walking and calling.

They helped all they could, but it was Joanda who found her. Lolly was sound asleep among the weeds along the bayou. Sound asleep and safely guarded, for there was old Trouble, lying beside her, his head resting on her pink sunbonnet.

"Time to go home, Nannie?" asked Lolly sleepily.

"Time to go home, sugar," said Joanda, hugging her close.

CHAPTER XI

A New Year

"I wish Uncle Shine would come," said Ricky. "It's New Year's."

"If he didn't come on Christmas, why would he come on New Year's?" asked Steve gruffly.

"I'll jest put on an extra plate," said Mama.

As if in answer to Ricky's wish, a horn sounded out front. The children ran out and soon came back, leading Uncle Shine by the hand.

"Can I be the uninvited guest?" he asked.

"You're plumb welcome any time," said Mama.

"Miz Shands sent us a big goose for Christmas," said Mavis. "Why didn't you come and help eat it?"

Uncle Shine did not answer. He looked around at the children and smiled.

Joanda found it easy to talk to him again.

"Miz Shands is so nice," she said. "She brought us presents —socks and tie for Daddy, apron for Mama, a doll for Lolly, ball and bat for Ricky, and books—*story books* for the rest of us. *I didn't know she'd give us all that!*"

"Miz Shands' goose is done et up, Uncle Shine," said Ricky. "You come too late."

"We don't feast on New Year's Day," said Mama. "All we got is black-eyed peas cooked with hog jowl. We don't like it much but . . ."

"I know," said Uncle Shine. "It's a good old Arkansas custom. *If you eat black-eyed peas on New Year's, you'll have plenty of money all the rest of the year.* My Ma—your grandma, Neva—always told us that to keep us from feelin' too hungry."

"Yes," said Mama. "In our family, we've never eaten anything else on the first day of the year. But I can't see it's brought us any money to brag about. Come, sit down, everybody."

Uncle Shine said his long and flowery grace. It didn't take long to eat the black-eyed peas and there was no dessert. After the meal, they all went into the front room. There, lighted up by the shining glass in the front door, stood Mama's new couch and one stuffed armchair. The bed had been moved back to make way for them.

Uncle Shine stared. "Can I sit down on a beautiful chair like this? Or, is it just to be looked at?"

"Sit down, sit down!" cried the children.

"See the new couch, too, Uncle Shine," said Joanda. "They

[146]

look just as purty as they did in Atkins' furniture store window, don't they?"

"A heap purtier," said Uncle Shine. "I could go to sleep in this easy chair without half tryin'. But instead of going to sleep . . . Here, Dave, is something for you." He handed him a man's bill-fold.

Daddy opened it, bewildered. "What's this? It's not mine."

"It's yours. It's some of that black-eyed pea money that Neva was talking about," said Uncle Shine.

"What do you mean?" asked Daddy.

"I hate to admit to a dark past," said Uncle Shine, "but among other things, I've been a cotton rustler. I stole a trailer load of cotton once . . ."

Joanda jumped up. "Oh!" she exclaimed. "I *knew* it was you!"

"Did you guess?" asked Uncle Shine with a smile. "Were *you* the only one smart enough to guess, Nannie? I thought some of these smart boy detectives who go to the movies every Saturday would catch me and put me in jail."

"You'd a gone to the Pen," said Steve severely.

"If I'd a been caught," said Uncle Shine, "but I wasn't. You see it was all in the family. When it's one of your kinfolk . . ."

Mama laughed.

"I saw you down by the by-o early that evenin'," said Joanda, "and I wondered what you were up to. Then I found the scales in your coat pocket . . ."

"You did?" asked Uncle Shine. "I sorta slipped up there."

"But I didn't tell anybody," said Joanda proudly. "I took

them out and dropped them . . ."

"And saved me from getting caught and going to the Pen," added Uncle Shine.

"But why . . . ?" began Daddy.

"It's to help pay for that new team of mules—the money I got from that cotton I stole," said Uncle Shine.

"What team of mules?"

"I've got a fine pair picked out for you," said Uncle Shine. "Among other things I used to be a mule trader and I know my mules. I tried to get them for Christmas but couldn't. The man's going to bring them here today. Their names are Blue and Red."

"I'll ride Blue," said Joanda.

"I'll ride Red," cried Steve.

"I'll ride 'em both!" shouted Ricky.

Uncle Shine explained that he had stored the cotton in a small shed on Big Charley's other farm, eight miles away.

"If you'd a sold that cotton right then, Dave," said Uncle Shine, "you'd a got less and the money woulda gone quicker. It was all a ruse to keep you from spending your cotton money. Neva and I wanted you to get your own mules."

"Thank you, Uncle," laughed Mama. "You took your life in your hands. I tried to keep you from being shot that night. I put the lamp in the window to warn you Dave was coming out with his shotgun."

"You should have seen me scoot!" laughed Uncle Shine.

"So it was *you* and not a chicken thief," said Joanda.

Uncle Shine put his hand under the girl's chin. "A cotton rustler's ten times worse than a chicken thief, sugar."

"Not when it's *all in the family*," said Joanda. "You're the nicest cotton rustler in the whole world." Lolly and Ricky jumped on Uncle Shine's lap and began to pull his beard.

A horn sounded out front.

"Now who's *that?*" cried Mama.

Daddy opened the door and in walked Big Charley, the bossman.

"Happy New Year, folks," he said. "I got good news for you, Dave. George Powell, the tenant on my farm in Promised Land, is moving to Tennessee. His wife wants to be nearer her kinfolk. Will you move into Powell's house and be my tenant?"

"You'll take *me*," gasped Daddy, "in George Powell's place? Why, he's been one of the best farmers round here."

"I sure will," said Big Charley. "I know a good man when I see one. You've gone ahead steadily in spite of setbacks. You're saving to get your own tools—I can help you till they're paid for—and . . ."

"And his own mules," added Uncle Shine.

"Uncle Shine has picked me out a team and I've got enough for the down payment on 'em," explained Daddy.

"Hooray!" shouted Ricky. "We're gonna move."

"We stayed *two years* in this old house," said Mama. "I'm right proud of that."

Joanda looked around at the newspaper-covered walls. She knew all the words and pictures on them by heart. She almost hated to leave them, but—maybe there'd be pretty wallpaper at the new tenant house. "Daddy, daddy! What about our glass door?"

"We'll take it with us," said Daddy.

"Here comes a truck with the mules," called Ricky.

The truck pulled up and the man unloaded the mules and drove off. The men examined the animals carefully. They lifted their hooves, looked into their mouths and patted their backs. Then Big Charley went away.

"There's only one thing," said Uncle Shine. "The owner told me Old Blue's a bit stubborn, but I never saw a good mule that wasn't."

Daddy patted Blue on the nose. "He'll be all right. Yes, he'll do."

"I want a ride! I want a ride!" begged the children.

"Mama, I want to ride Old Blue," begged Joanda.

"You'll smell like a mule if you do," said Mama. "You'll git black hairs all over you."

"I don't care," insisted Joanda. "I want a ride."

Daddy helped them up, Joanda on Blue and Steve on Red. They rode the mules around the house and down the road. Steve turned around, came back and took Ricky up behind him. But Old Blue kept on going. Joanda pulled on the bridle rein, but Old Blue refused to turn.

"Mama, Mama!" called the girl.

Mama stood on the porch and laughed. "You're ridin' Old Blue. That's what you wanted."

Steve and Ricky rode round the house on Red, then they started up the road to the Burgesses. Mavis wanted a ride on Blue and kept calling.

But Blue had his own ideas. He crossed the cotton patch and walked up on the bayou bank. Then, with Joanda cling-

ing tightly, he went down the steep slope into the water. He
took a long drink, waded farther out and stopped.

Joanda pulled her legs up, but they were already wet. She
sat very stiff and still, afraid she would fall into the cold water.
She waited but nobody came. She pulled the reins and spoke
to the mule: "Giddap, Blue. Giddap. Let's go home." She
begged and scolded and coaxed, but Old Blue just stood there.

Joanda felt sure somebody would come for her soon. But
no one came. Minutes that seemed hours passed. Her legs,
covered only by thin blue jeans, grew stiff and cold. A north
wind chilled her. She had run out of the house without a
sweater.

It began to grow dark and she became frightened. *Why
didn't some one come?*

Then she saw them—the whole family standing on the bank

in a row, laughing at her. Joanda's face turned red. She knew they would tease her to death about this.

"Daddy's gone for a boat to bring you in," shouted Steve.

Down the bayou came Daddy in a rowboat he had borrowed from the Burgess boys. Closer and closer he came, till he was right under Old Blue's nose. "Throw me the reins, Nannie," he said.

He fastened them to the boat and rowed to shore. Old Blue followed meekly. Joanda jumped off into Daddy's arms. He set her on the ground.

"Mama," said Joanda, "now I smell like a mule and I've got black hairs all over me."

Mama laughed. "You rode Old Blue—that's what you wanted. Come home now and have a hot bath, before you ketch your death of cold."

*   *   *

"Where do I put this, Mama?" Joanda held up a pink glass pitcher.

"Pack it in the bushel basket with the other dishes," said Mama, "so it won't git broke."

The Hutleys were getting ready to move. The Powell place was in Promised Land on the other side of town, about eight miles away. But the children would still attend Delta Flats School, being transported by bus.

They moved on a Saturday. J. T. and Aunt Lessie came over, and all the children helped. Mama could not do any heavy lifting, so it was Aunt Lessie who wrapped old quilts about the furniture, to prevent scratching. Daddy had already hauled the mules and his new farm machinery over. He took Mavis and Steve on the first load of furniture and came back for the second.

After the table, couch, armchair and dishes had been put in, Daddy took off the glass front door and replaced the old wooden one. He tied the glass door inside the truck railing.

Then it was time to go.

Aunt Lessie held out her arms and Mama and Joanda kissed her. The women cried and Joanda could not keep the tears back. They felt as if they were going on a long journey.

"We can't run in as often as we used to," said Aunt Lessie.

Mama took Lolly in her arms. "It's only eight miles. We'll come to see you and you come to see us." She paused, groping for words. "We can still be neighbors . . . I . . . I couldn't a made out without you. . . ."

Aunt Lessie just smiled.

The men shook hands and Daddy drove off.

Joanda looked back. Outside the place looked just the same. There was the empty goose run at the side and the two tire rims that had protected the two zinnia beds. There was the black spot where the coal used to be piled, and there were tin cans and bottles lying about. There was the goose pump out front.

But the red shotgun house was empty now. It was shabby and run-down, and it had never been large enough for their needs. Now the beautiful glass door was gone, and the house was shorn of its glory, shorn of life, of all those varying activities of a group of human beings which could make of so shabby a building a home.

Joanda felt sorry to go.

Then she looked at Daddy. Somehow he seemed different. He was no longer a sharecropper, but a tenant. She took comfort in the thought and her heart beat high with hope.

As they drove toward town on the highway, they noticed that the grass and weeds along the sides were being burned off.

"Best time o' year to do that, in winter," said Daddy. "It will kill the weed seeds and the eggs of weevils and other pests. All the weeds are good and dry now—they'll burn easy."

"If it was in cotton-pickin' time," said Mama, "it'd be dangerous. It might could set fire to the loads of cotton bein' hauled in."

"Yes, if there was a wind like today," said Daddy.

Lolly began to chatter:

"Rabbit skip, rabbit hop,
Rabbit bit my turnip top . . ."

"Daddy!" cried Joanda, sniffing. "I smell something burnin'."

Daddy laughed. "You're smellin' that grass and them weeds," he said.

"No," said Joanda. "It smells like cloth."

"Likely somebody threw an old rag in the ditch," said Mama.

Ricky pointed. "There it is. I see a rag a-burnin'."

They rode happily on, Lolly repeating her verse over and over. When they came into town they passed Uncle Shine's house.

"Oh, I wish Uncle Shine could see us movin'!" cried Joanda.

But the house was closed up and no one was there.

They came to Main Street, the street down which Joanda had ridden so many Saturdays, standing in the back of the truck. No one had ever noticed their truck—it was just like all the others. But today the people were pointing. Joanda was thrilled. The Hutleys were important today because they were moving. The people were pointing to the nice new furniture in the back of the Hutleys' truck.

Then suddenly Joanda cried out: "They're sayin' *fire!* They mean *us!*"

But Daddy wouldn't believe it. "Fire?" he said. "Somebody's house on fire. I sure hope the fire truck won't come along Main Street till we can git out of the way."

"You don't think . . ." began Mama.

"It's *US!*" cried Joanda, standing up and looking back. *"Our furniture's on fire. The quilts are burnin' up!"*

"Those weeds!" gasped Mama.

Both sides of the street were filled with parked cars. Daddy had to keep going till he could find a place to turn out a little. By that time, the whole back of the truck was ablaze. Daddy pulled the brake and they got out.

Mama took Lolly and tried to quiet her screams. "It caught from the grass fire along the side of the road," she explained to the people who crowded up. "We never even knew it . . ."

"Water! Git water!" Joanda stood in the street and shouted. "Can't you see our new furniture is burnin' *up?*"

But the people just stood there. Nobody did anything.

Joanda ran into the nearest cafe. *"Water!"* she gasped. *"I want water!"*

The tables and counter were crowded with people waiting to be served, but the waiter heard her and quickly handed her a paper cup of water.

"Three cents!" he said.

"Three cents?" cried Joanda. Her red purse hung on her arm. "You charge three cents for water?"

"Three cents I said, and I mean it!" repeated the waiter angrily. Then seeing the girl's face, he added, "All right, two then."

Joanda fumbled in her purse for the money and handed it to him, trying not to spill the cup of water. All the people were looking at her.

"What d'you mean—chargin' for water?" she demanded, starting for the door.

"Water's free," called the waiter. "Two cents for the cup."

Outside, Joanda ran to the burning truck. She threw the water, paper cup and all, to the ground in disgust. Then she saw a large fat man pulling at one leg of Mama's table.

Joanda kicked him sharply on the shins. "You let that table alone," she said. "You can't have it. Can't you see you're pullin' it to pieces?" It was tied to the truck so it wouldn't fall out.

"It's on fire!" said the man. He stopped pulling the table and took hold of the arm of the new couch. He climbed up and handed a small chair over the side railing. A thin man took it.

"You jest let our furniture alone," cried Joanda. She glanced at the truck. Armchair and table were blazing. The flames were leaping to the smaller chairs. The fat man had taken a

[158]

quilt and was beating it on the armchair.

"Come on, get outa here!" A policeman appeared, waving his club. "Get this truck outa here!" he ordered. "Drive down to that gas station and git water to put your fire out."

"Not till that man puts our chair back!" cried Joanda, pointing.

Angrily, the thin man threw the chair back onto the truck. It fell against the glass door with a loud crash, shattering the glass to pieces.

"*He broke the glass in our front door!*" cried Joanda.

But Daddy was driving off to the gas station, and Mama, with Lolly in her arms and Ricky hanging to her skirt, was following through the crowd. Joanda ran after them.

The gas station man had a garden hose. He began to sprinkle water on the burning pieces.

"Stop that, mister! You're gittin' it *wet!*" cried Joanda.

"Quickest way to put out a fire, sister," answered the man.

In a few minutes the fire was out.

Joanda stared at the crowd that had gathered. Then she remembered. It was Saturday—that's why the town was so full of farmers and their families. She hated all the strange faces. *Take a good look*, she said to herself, *you've got something to see this time. This is one Saturday you'll git your money's worth. You'll talk about it all the way home and for weeks afterwards. You'll talk about the Hutleys and how their new furniture burned up.*

Joanda felt sick and ashamed. For the first time, as if she had held up a mirror, she saw the Hutleys as they really were. She saw her family from the outside, as if she were a stranger.

[159]

The Hutleys were messy and untidy. Lolly's face was dirty from crying and Mama's hair was blowing. Mama looked like an old, old woman since she had her teeth pulled out. Daddy's face and arms were black with soot. Ricky needed a haircut and his overalls were torn.

Joanda looked down at herself. She was the worst of them all. She was black from the soot and wet from the water. She had lost the scarf she wore on her head, and her hair hung loose over her face. She hadn't combed it that morning.

A wave of shame engulfed her.

Then she heard Daddy talking.

"I'm almost glad it happened, Neva," he said cheerfully. "Now we can git us some *new* furniture!"

"*New* furniture?" gasped Mama.

Was Daddy crazy? No—Joanda knew he was just trying to make Mama feel better, but suddenly she felt enraged. She could hold in her fury no longer.

"*New* furniture?" she repeated. "Don't say that again or I'll hit you. You know this ain't all paid for, Daddy. *Where we gonna git the money to pay for more?*"

Then some one took her by the shoulders and gave her a good shaking. A voice said sharply: "Hush up, Joanda. I'm shocked at you. Making a scene in the street like this. I thought you had more sense."

Through her tears, Joanda saw a woman with a hat on and recognized Mrs. Shands. *What's the boss-man's wife know about it? She's never had her new furniture to burn up! She's still got her purple couch! What business has she got shakin' me to pieces?* And there was Uncle Shine too. *His house is*

full o' purty furniture. He never had nothin' to burn up . . .
Mrs. Shands and Uncle Shine were smiling as if nothing had
happened at all. It made the girl madder to look at them both.

"I been out to Promised Land to see that tenant house o'
yours," Uncle Shine was saying. "You're gonna like it. Why,
it's got five rooms instead of three, Nannie. Think of that!"

They drove on out to the new house, about three miles east
of town, on a side road that cut through to Big Charley's other
farm. The house was square, box-shaped, with a small cut-
under front porch. The yard was larger and had three mul-
berry trees. There were barns, pig-pens and sheds at the back,
and a place for a vegetable garden.

Joanda cried when they unloaded the truck. The seat of the
new couch was soaked with water. Its cloth covering was
badly burned. Both arms of the stuffed armchair were burned
off. The table and one small chair had to be thrown away.
Others were scarred and black.

Mavis and Mama cried too.

Daddy took the tenant house door off its hinges and fitted
the glass door in place.

"Broken glass! That sure looks purty!" cried Joanda bitterly. "What we want glass in our front door for anyhow?
To see our burnt furniture?" She sat down on the front step
and buried her face in her hands.

Daddy began to whistle cheerfully. "Don't you know I'm
a carpenter, Nannie? I'll put a new glass in this door and I'll
repair that furniture so you won't know what happened to it."

Mavis began to unpack the dishes. "Mama, the pink pitcher
didn't git broke."

"That's lucky," said Mama. "It cost a dollar forty-nine at the dime store."

"Mama," called Mavis again. "Ain't the wallpaper purty?"

"Sure is," answered Mama. But Joanda did not go in to see it.

Mrs. Shands drove up in her car. She went into the house without speaking to Joanda. She made Mama lie down on the first bed that was set up. She helped Mavis and Daddy arrange the furniture.

"We'll leave the couch on the front porch till it dries out," said Mrs. Shands. "I have some old drapes at home just that same color. We can use them to cover up the burned places . . . Just as soon as Charley gets ahead a little, we want to put electric lights in this house for you. Then you won't need these lamps . . . You'll have to have some new curtains, Neva. We've got plenty of feed sacks in pretty patterns and colors . . . I'll teach Joanda to sew on my electric sewing machine . . ."

Joanda listened dully to the things Mrs. Shands was saying. Like Daddy, she was just saying nice things so Mama wouldn't feel so bad about the fire.

Joanda wondered if she could ever care about anything again.

CHAPTER XII

The Bridge

"Hurry, Ricky, or we'll miss the bus," called Joanda. She tied her scarf tightly under her chin and buttoned her coat. Ricky came running out of the house behind her.

Going to school was exciting now, for it meant catching the school bus each morning. Mavis and Steve went to Junior High this year, so they took the bus a half hour earlier on its way into town.

The two children ran down the road and came to the bridge over the bayou. It was the same Pemiscot Bayou that they had known so well when they lived in the red shotgun house. The bridge was old and rickety and many of the boards were coming loose. Ricky knelt down and peeked through a hole. "Golly! the water's high!" he said.

"Come on," said Joanda, "we'll be late."

When they reached the corner, the bus had not come. They waited under the shed there. The sky looked dark and threatening.

"I think it's gonna snow," said Ricky. "If it does, I'll make me a snow man."

"More rain," said Joanda. "Daddy says we always have too much rain in the spring. Sometimes they have floods along the Mississippi River and the people in the river bottoms have to move out. There, it's sprinkling again."

"Will it wash our house away?" asked Ricky.

"No," said Joanda. "We live on high ground and we're twenty miles from the Mississippi River. Just so that old by-o don't git to actin' up."

The bus came along and they got on. The driver, Ed Haley,

called, "Hi, there, young uns. Half an hour late today. Had to jump so many mud-puddles. Now if this old bus just had webbed feet like a duck so it could swim . . ."

The children laughed. The bus jerked along, slipping and sliding over the muddy road. The ditches were so deep on both sides, Joanda was afraid the bus might slide down the bank. She sat stiff with fear.

"Bring your fishin' pole, Ricky?" cried Ed. "Just seen a big catfish in that mud-puddle!"

"I forgot it, Ed," answered Ricky. "I'll sure bring it to-morrow."

The children laughed—all but Joanda. When they finally got to school, she was glad. She and Ricky no longer carried cold lunches. Uncle Shine paid for their hot lunches and they ate with the other children. Joanda liked being with Miss Fenton all day.

Today a wonderful thing happened. Miss Fenton put Joanda in charge of the library books. She was to check out the books for the children to take home. And Miss Fenton told her how to mark off the books when they were returned.

"What if something happens to a book and they can't return it?" Joanda hung her head when she asked the question.

"They'll report it and we'll understand," said Miss Fenton. "When we lose a book, we'll remember the happiness it gave its readers and we will try to replace it." She paused. "You will make a good librarian because you love books and take such good care of them."

She trusts me, thought Joanda. *Miss Fenton trusts me with all the books even though 1 lost one of them.* She felt happy all the way through, and from that day, the other children looked upon her with new respect.

It was still raining when school was dismissed. Ed Haley honked the horn of the school bus noisily.

"Got to git goin'," he said as the children climbed in. "Don't want to git drownded out on the way home. Bring your fishin' pole, Ricky?"

The bus left the highway and began its rough rocking over the side roads where most of the children lived. Ed drove carefully while his passengers sat still and strangely quiet. The rain pounded against the windows and the windshield wiper groaned as it moved back and forth. Joanda sat sober-faced and serious. She wished they were walking, the way they used to when they lived in the shotgun house.

Suddenly Ricky burst out: "That ditch is so big, when it gits full of water, somebody might could git drownded!"

"Not while Old Ed is at the wheel," called the driver. But he did not look around or start joking.

They passed a boy trudging along the road barefoot, his shoes tied by strings hanging around his neck. There was no traffic on the road and all the houses looked deserted. The people were keeping dry inside. Ed made frequent stops to let the children get off.

The Hutleys and the Banister children, Alice and Bill, had the farthest to go. About two miles from the Hutleys' house, the bus engine sputtered and stopped.

"Here we are!" said Ed, cheerfully. "Safe in the middle of the road and *not* in the ditch."

"What'll we do, Ed?" asked Bill Banister. "Git out and walk?"

"Let's wait a while," said Ed. "I think somebody will come for us. Who knows some games?"

Joanda started *Do You Chew Tobacco* and then they tried to play *May I?* and *Sugarloaf Town*, but there weren't enough children and the bus wasn't big enough. After they grew tired, Joanda recited:

> " '*Way down on Grandpa's farm,*
> *Billy goat chased me round the barn;*
> *Chased me up the sycamore tree,*
> *And this is what he said to me:*
> *I like apples, I like tea,*
> *How many little boys are stuck on me?*
> *One, two three . . .* ' "

Just then a rap came at the bus door, and there was Dave Hutley, riding Blue and leading Red.

"We guessed you must be stuck when the kids didn't come home," he said. "Mr. Banister is down at the crossroad in his truck."

Daddy took Alice and Bill to their father first, then he took Ed Haley because Mr. Banister had offered to run him back to town. At last he came for Ricky and Joanda.

"I won't ride old stubborn Blue," said Joanda.

"I'll take Ricky with me and you can ride Red," said Daddy. "Red's always gentle and never balks."

The rain slackened and the mules stepped carefully along the soft mud road. When they reached the bridge over the bayou, Old Blue balked.

"No wonder," said Daddy. "That mule's got sense. The bridge is so rotten, it's not safe any more." He got down and led the mules across. "Somebody's gonna fall through this bridge one of these days, then maybe the highway department will fix it."

They got safely home that day, little dreaming how soon Daddy's prophetic words would come true. School was closed for two days until the rains stopped and the roads dried off. Then the sun came out again—a warm spring sun, bringing with it the tender budding of the trees and the fresh green of growing grass.

With spring came the rush of spring work, which meant many days' absence from school. Joanda mourned, wondering how the school library was getting along without her. But she could not go because to Mama and Daddy, farm work came first. A tenant farmer, as much as a sharecropper, needed the help of his children. They were considered "hands," as necessary as the mules or the machinery.

Life at the new home had not changed much, except that there was more work to do. Daddy bought seeds and planted a vegetable garden. Mama began raising baby chicks and young pigs which needed regular tending.

As in the old days, Daddy had no cash in hand. But it was easier now to get "furnish"—a loan for living expenses—from the White Top gin, because he had tools and mules, only partially paid for but representing an investment of six hundred dollars, to offer as security. As a tenant he still had to get furnished. He went to the gin for payments on the first and fifteenth of each month. He would borrow at 8% interest until the cotton crop came in.

The house was better and not so crowded. There was room

enough for all the furniture, but there was no electricity or running water. Wallpaper was pasted on the unplastered wood walls, but in the upper corners it was badly stained by leaks. Big Charley promised a new roof if Daddy would put on the roofing paper.

Daddy had a better contract with Big Charley. He would pay him one-fourth of the cotton and ten dollars an acre for land not in cotton. He was expected to rotate his crops, planting not more than 60 per cent in cotton, and the rest in alfalfa hay, corn and soy beans.

The work on the cotton was just the same except that Daddy was using his own tools instead of the boss-man's. He still had the use of Big Charley's tractor on his own acreage and Big Charley's; and the chance for extra pay from day labor done for Charley or at carpentry. When he couldn't have the tractor, he could use his mules.

On one of the first warm spring days, Joanda sat sewing on the front porch and watching her little sister.

"Nannie, take me to the store and buy me some candy," begged Lolly.

"Oh, stop teasin'," said Joanda. "You pester me to death."

"I want a candy bar . . . I want . . ." began Lolly.

"I'll wear you out if you say that once more," said Joanda. "I've got work to do. Can't you see I'm sewin' buttons on your new dress—the one I made on Miz Shands' sewin' machine?"

"I want candy," persisted Lolly. "I wanna go to the store."

"Why don't you play like you're a grown-up lady and go to the store and buy your own candy?"

"I got me a nickel," said Lolly proudly, patting her pocket.

She ran around the house, singing happily. Joanda finished her sewing, then brought the rest of the clothes in off the line and sprinkled them. Mama was busy at the ironing board.

"You'd better take water out to the field, Nannie," said Mama. "Daddy will be gittin' thirsty. If you see Lolly, tell her to come in here to me."

Joanda put her sunbonnet on, pumped a bucket of water and started off over the field.

Daddy was planting corn. Forty acres was considered "a family crop," or a "two-mule farm," that being the acreage that a team of mules could handle. The mules would be used for only part of the year, for plowing and cultivating, but they would have to be fed all the year round. So Daddy was planting enough corn for the mules and for a surplus of about fifty bushels to sell.

Joanda walked slowly across the newly-plowed field. The sun had real warmth in it now. It felt good to know that summer would soon be here.

"Have you seen Lolly anywhere?" Joanda asked.

"No, Nannie," said Daddy, drinking from the dipper.

"Who's that screaming?" cried Joanda.

"It must be them colored people down on the by-o fishing," said Daddy. "First warm day brings 'em all out. Likely somebody's caught a catfish. Sounds like they're havin' 'em a good time."

"There's Steve callin', Daddy," said Joanda.

At the edge of the bushes along the bayou, Steve had been cutting weeds. Now he stood waving and calling. Daddy jumped off the planter.

"I'll go see what he's found," he said. "Might be a water moccasin. You stay here, Nannie, and hold the mules. They're still skittish and might could run away." He hurried across the field in long strides.

It's Lolly, thought Joanda. *I just know something's happened to Lolly.* Ricky had been with Steve. Now she saw Ricky come to meet Daddy and run back with him to the bayou. *I bet Lolly's fell in the by-o. I told her to go to the store and buy candy and I bet that's what she did.*

There was nothing Joanda could do but stand in the field and hold the mules. She could still hear screams, but could see nothing. *She's fell in and drownded before Daddy got there and it's all my fault.*

Joanda waited a long time. Then she saw people walking

along the road. They had crossed over the bayou bridge and were walking slowly toward the Hutley house. Somebody was being carried on Daddy's shoulder and Joanda knew without being told that it was Lolly.

She saw Mama and Mavis come running out to meet Daddy. Then they all disappeared inside the square green house.

The tears rolled down Joanda's face.

She wanted to go to Lolly, but she knew she must mind Daddy and hold the mules. Blue was standing quietly, but Red was getting restless. It would only make things worse if the mules ran away. She waited a long time. At last Daddy came out for her in the truck. He brought Steve along and Steve took charge of the mules because he was learning to drive them.

"Git in, Nannie," said Daddy.

"Is she drownded?" asked Joanda, her face white with fear.

"No, Nannie, but it was a close shave." Daddy told what had happened. "I got there just in time. Of all them colored people fishin'—seventeen of 'em—not one could swim. Jim Healy saved her. He waded in up to his neck and brought her out. The water's so high, must be fifteen feet deep under that bridge. If I'd a had the highest pole in the world I couldn'ta found the bottom of it.

"There she was floatin', her skirt holdin' her up. Jim said she stayed on the water a real long time before she went under. They all said she stayed on the top of the water longer than any one they ever saw. Sally, Jim's wife, thought she was swimmin'. She went down twice, then somehow she got hold of a bush along the side and held onto it. The women were screamin' *Lord have mercy! Lord have mercy!* when Jim walked in after her . . .

"I pulled off my shoes, and I wanted to take my overalls off, but I was afraid I wouldn't have time. She'd gone down twice and come up again. But Jim had her. He got holt of her skirt and pulled her to shore, and I jest lifted her out. I'm sure glad Jim Healy went fishin' this mornin' . . ."

"Is she all right?" whispered Joanda.

"She's purty weak, but she's all right," said Daddy. "I got all the water out of her lungs. Mama and I can't understand what she was doin' down there. She never run so far from home before."

Joanda said nothing.

"Jim's wife, Sally, said she was on her way to the store to spend a nickel," Daddy went on. "She marched across the bridge so big, sayin', 'I'm a big lady! I'm goin' to the store to buy me some candy!' The colored people laughed at her, she was so cute, they said. That bridge's got so many holes in it —she wasn't lookin' where she was goin' and her foot caught in one. The board was rotten and broke, and down she went and they began to scream."

I should have watched her, thought Joanda. *I should have kept her with me. Oh, why did I tell her to go to the store?*

They were back at the house now and Joanda was afraid to go in. Jim and Sally Healy and the other Negroes were still there. They were looking at Lolly lying there on the bed in the bedroom. They were praying to the Lord in long prayers to save her. Joanda went in and saw her. She came quickly out again.

"She looks like she's dead," Joanda said and shivered.

"Law no, she don't," said Sally Healy. "Her color's comin' back fast and her hands and feet are warm. When Jim first pulled her out, she was white as a ghost. She'll be runnin' around by tomorrow."

"We better let her sleep now," said Mama.

"You white folks keep these fish," said Jim Healy, handing over a string of catfish and crappie.

"Jim, we oughta give *you* somethin' for what you done," said Mama. "What if you hadn't been there?"

"Jim," said Daddy, shaking his hand. "You saved our baby for us."

Jim nodded. "I got a baby myself."

"And you're soaked to the skin like me," said Daddy. "We'll have to put on dry clothes."

"She'll be all right now, don't you white folks worry now," said Sally as they went out the door.

After Daddy changed his clothes, he said: "Looky here. I've ruined my pocket watch, my money and everything. Just got our half-months' 'furnish' yesterday and now look at it. My watch won't run—it's soaked with by-o water."

"I'll spread the bills out by the stove to dry 'em," said Mama. "Your watch will have to dry out and be oiled again. Why, Nannie, what are you cryin' about?"

Joanda sat on a chair by the kitchen table. She wouldn't look up or answer.

"Nannie, what's the matter?" begged Daddy. "It's all over now. Lolly's all right. She'll be as good as new once she gets a good sleep. She's all *right*, I tell you."

"I know, but . . ."

Joanda couldn't tell them. That night in bed, she began crying again. Mama came and sat by her and at last she was able to find the words:

"Lolly asked me to take her to the store and I wouldn't go," said Joanda brokenly. "I told her to go herself . . . and she did . . ."

"*Nannie! Nannie!*" A little voice called from the next room.

"It's Lolly!" cried Joanda. "She wants me."

In bare feet and nightgown, Joanda flew to her little sister, who was sitting up in bed. She took her in her arms and held her close.

"She's all right again, Mama!"

*   *   *

Summer flew by on wings.

Once again the cotton was planted and came up, and school was dismissed. Cotton chopping came and went, more quickly this year for the help of the boss-man's geese. On the Fourth of July, traditional "laying-by time" in the cotton country, Daddy planned a fish-fry in a favorite spot along the shore of the Mississippi River. The Burgesses, the Shands and the Suttons came, all ready for a good time.

The picnic grounds overlooked an old wrecked pier, which had once been a scene of busy activity when cotton was loaded onto river boats. The water in the great river was smooth, but kept moving fast downstream. Driftwood and sand were banked against breakwaters. The shore was tree-covered, shady and pleasant.

The men borrowed boats, put their nets out and caught minnows for bait. Then they took the boys and went fishing. The girls and younger children waded along the sandy shore, while the women sat and visited. When the men brought the fish in and began to clean them, the women started fires in the charcoal buckets. Mrs. Burgess placed wire racks over the buckets and began to fry the fish. The other women set out the rest of the food—cornbread, potato chips, onions, pickles and iced tea.

Uncle Shine turned up at the last minute. "Am I in time for the fish fry? Can I fry the fish?" Aunt Lessie handed him the fork and Joanda tied an apron round his waist. Soon the platter was piled high with hot fish.

The Suttons brought a two-gallon freezer for ice cream and Maggie called Bug Burgess and Steve Hutley to turn it by hand. There were two large layer cakes to be eaten with the ice cream.

"Come on, everybody! Come and eat!"

CHAPTER XIII

Another Saturday

O*h, it's Saturday—beautiful Saturday!* The minute she woke up, Joanda felt happy all over. It was October again, cotton-picking time. But nobody picked on Saturdays. They always went to town.

There was the same old scramble of getting ready—washing faces and ears, combing hair and putting on fresh clean clothes. There was the same rush to the waiting truck, the same throbbing of the engine shaking it back and forth. Mama and Daddy took Lolly into the cab with them, and the other children rode standing in the back.

The truck bounced and bumped over the dirt road until it came to the smooth highway. The sun shone warm on the children's backs and the wind blew through their hair. Then town, and riding through Main Street in the long parade of cars and trucks. Joanda could see everything—the cars, the crowds of people, the stores. But no one on the sidewalks noticed the Hutleys at all.

Daddy parked in his old place behind the Beehive store and they all climbed down. They walked together to Main Street and they did what they always did first. They just looked. They were all happy because they had money in their pockets to spend, money earned by picking cotton. And the show-windows and sidewalks were full of wonderful, tempting things.

"It's nice to think what you'd like to buy," said Mama, "even if you don't buy it."

Joanda pressed her nose against a store window pane. *I can have that, I can have that if I want it*, she thought to herself.

The pattern of this Saturday was like hundreds of other Saturdays in the past. The Hutleys always went to the same places and did the same things, and each week enjoyed them as if for the very first time.

"Where's the hot tamale man?" asked Ricky. "I'd buy a hot tamale today if only it wouldn't burn my tongue."

"Where's the blind man?" asked Mavis. "I don't see him anywhere."

"I want to hear purty music," cried Lolly, running on ahead.

"You come right back here, young lady," cried Joanda, "or I'll sure blister you."

They came to the Star Movie Theater, which had not opened yet, and stopped to look at the scenes from the current picture.

"It sure looks good and exciting," said Mavis.

"That fellow there's the villain," Steve pointed out. "See his six-shooter?"

"When I know who's the outlaw and who's shootin' who . . ." Mavis began.

Joanda shivered. "I don't want to see it if there's shootin' in it."

They came to the popcorn stand and Daddy said, "Let's have some popcorn." So he bought seven sacks, one for each, and they stood and ate it. Ricky ate two sacks in the time the others ate one. Lolly choked on hers and spilled the rest over the sidewalk. Then she cried for more.

"I'll git my new teeth the very first thing," said Mama. "Dave, you come in the dentist's office with me. You kids wait out here." After a while, Mama and Daddy came out again.

"Golly, Mama," said Steve, "I hardly know you."

"They look fine, Mama," said Mavis. "Smile for us."

Mama smiled.

"You look purty," said Joanda, "and young too."

Mama and Daddy laughed.

"Mama," began Mavis, "I think you and I should git permanents. Nannie's too young, she don't need one."

"If Mavis gits one, I want one too," begged Joanda.

Mama looked at the two girls. "We'll all three give up our permanents, because my teeth took all the extra money. You want to help save, don't you?"

The girls nodded.

"We'll buy the home-made kind and do them at home," said Mama. "Let's go to the clothing store."

[179]

Each fall they had to have new clothes, so they went to the Beehive and bought dresses for the girls and pants and shirts for the boys, and new shoes all around. Then Daddy said, "Well, I reckon I'll just mosey along . . ."

"We'll go to the bank first," said Mama.

"That's right," said Daddy with a smile. "I almost forgot."

The children waited outside. They had never been in a bank and they felt a strange awe for this great building of marble where you could keep your money safe.

When Mama and Daddy came out, Mama said, "We'll wait for you at the Goodwill, Dave. Let's try and git home early tonight."

"Sure, let's do that," said Daddy as he walked off.

Steve and Mavis met the Burgess children and went back to wait for the Star Theater to open. Joanda kept tight hold of Lolly on one side and Ricky on the other. It was in front of the Goodwill that they met Miss Fenton. Joanda hadn't seen her since the split-term summer session had closed in August.

"Hello, Miss Fenton," said Joanda.

"Hello, Miss Fenton," said Ricky.

"I hear you are going to have a home of your own, Mrs. Hutley," said the teacher.

"Why, who told you?" asked Mama.

"I just met Mrs. Shands down the street," said Miss Fenton. "Is it true?"

"Some day, we hope," said Mama.

"Mama wants it to be a brick house with a concrete storm cellar," said Joanda. "It's gonna be our *permanent* home, the kind you never move away from. It's gonna *last forever*."

Miss Fenton smiled.

"Mama wants it to be a pusher-button house," added Ricky.

"Hush, Ricky," said Mama. "You're tellin' all my secrets."

Miss Fenton laughed. "I hope there will be lots of buttons to push," she said. "We all have our dreams, Mrs. Hutley."

"Now that we're tenants," explained Mama, "we hope to lay a little by each year, to start payments on a little place of our own."

"Uncle Shine says he'll find it for us," said Joanda. "Uncle Shine used to be a lightning-rod salesman and a mule trader and a cotton rustler . . ."

"Hush, Nannie," said Mama. "My uncle's a good man, Miss Fenton. He has helped us git ahead a little. If it hadn't been for him, we'd still be sharecroppers."

"I'm glad," said Miss Fenton.

"If we can find a little place," said Mama, "we'll have to pay one-third down, about two thousand dollars, then the rest like rent. That's an awful lot of money and it'll take us the rest of our lives, I reckon."

"Not if you are careful," said Miss Fenton. "Not if you really want a home and are willing to make sacrifices."

"Dave don't want to be a rich owner," Mama went on. "He don't want to be a boss-man and hire and fire tenants and share-croppers—he knows how it feels to be one himself. So it will jest be a small place. We'll raise jest what we need to live on, and three or four bales of cotton extry for a little cash. We'll plant alfalfa and soybeans too, but we won't git more land than we can take care of ourselves."

"I think that's a good idea," said Miss Fenton. "And meanwhile you'll stay on in Charley Shands' tenant house?"

"Yes ma'm," said Mama. "We're lucky to be in it, even if it does leak."

"It's got purty wallpaper," said Joanda, "and Miz Shands let me make feed-sack curtains on her 'lectric sewing machine."

"What about the furniture that got burned?" asked Miss Fenton. "I was sorry to hear about that."

"Miz Shands gave me some old drapes and I patched the upholstery," said Mama. "Dave made new arms for the armchair and we bought a new table. Steve and Mavis painted the other chairs. So we're makin' out."

"I'll tell you another secret, Miss Fenton," said Joanda. "Mama's got her new teeth today. Don't she look purty? But she can't have a permanent—it's too expensive."

"Hush, Nannie," said Mama, her face turning red. "You talk too much. I figured I had to have the teeth, Miss Fenton, but I'd give the cost of the permanent to our new home."

"We can give ourselves home permanents," said Joanda, "like you did at school."

Miss Fenton smiled and nodded. "Speaking of secrets," she said, "I'm going to tell you my secret dream. I want a better library at Delta Flats School and we are starting to raise the money for it ourselves."

"Oh!" said Mama. "I'm afraid we can't help . . . I had to pay for my teeth today, and I've talked Dave into puttin' all our crop money in the bank for a start on that down payment . . . There's still some to be paid on the mules . . . and he'll have to git a tractor . . ."

"I know you can't give money," said Miss Fenton, "but

maybe you can give a little time. We thought we'd have a cotton-picking picnic and we are inviting everybody to come and pick half a day for the school."

Joanda clapped her hands. "Children too?"

"Of course, children too," said Miss Fenton. "They'll read the books, so they'll want to help earn them. And so many of the children are expert pickers. George Barclay has offered to let us pick in that large field of his next to the school. It grows some of the finest cotton in the county. He will pay regular picking wages for what we pick, and it will all be donated to the school for the library fund."

"When it's for the school, everybody helps," said Mama.

"Mama's about the fastest woman picker in the county, Miss Fenton . . ."

"Oh hush, Nannie," said Mama. "I used to be purty good, but my pickin' days are over. The doctor won't let me now, on account of my bad heart. That's made it hard for Dave. But we'll come to the picnic and the rest of the family can pick."

"You can help with the supper, Mrs. Hutley," said Miss Fenton. "George Barclay is giving a hog for a barbecue."

"Goody, goody! Pig sandwiches!" cried Ricky.

"We sure did like those books that Nannie brought home," said Mama.

"You'll like the new ones too," said Miss Fenton.

After Miss Fenton went away, Mama went in the store and there she met Mrs. Shands.

"I been wantin' to see you, Miz Shands," said Mama in a low voice.

"Is anything wrong, Neva?"

"No, but . . . Well, I heard Dave a-talkin' to Uncle Shine," said Mama. "You know we're fixin' to git a little place of our own."

Mrs. Shands nodded and her face saddened. "We'll hate to lose you," she said.

"You will?" exclaimed Mama. "Then you're not studyin' to throw us out?"

"What do you mean, Neva?" asked Mrs. Shands. "Charley never throws a man out unless he breaks his contract."

"I heard Dave a-tellin' Uncle Shine that bein' a tenant is no better than bein' a sharecropper," said Mama. "He said any time a better tenant comes along, the boss-man can throw a tenant and his family out and take on the better man. It sounded as if Big Charley had found somebody and was fixin' to put him in our house."

Mrs. Shands laughed. "Well, I never! Just when we've been worryin' over losing you because you are starting to pay for a place of your own. Charley was wondering what we could do to keep you satisfied and I told him quick: new roof, running water and electric lights, and he said: 'That's right. We've got to find a way to do it, to keep a man like Dave.'"

The two women laughed.

"Guess we'll have to begin to trust each other," said Mrs. Shands.

"And help each other," added Mama. "You needn't to worry about us leavin'. We ain't found our little place yet and it'll take a heap o' years to save enough for that down payment. And still more years to pay off the balance."

"We won't worry," said Mrs. Shands. "We'll help you all we can. I know what it means to have a place all your own and *all paid for*."

"It's gonna be a pusher-button house, Miz Shands," said Joanda.

"And I'm gonna push all the buttons!" added Ricky.

Mrs. Shands laughed. "Well, I must go look for Charley," she said.

After Mrs. Shands left, Mama and the children went to the lunch counter in the Goodwill and had hamburgers and cold drinks.

"Where's Lolly?" cried Joanda, looking around suddenly.

"You go hunt for her, Nannie," said Mama. "It wouldn't be a good Saturday in town if Lolly didn't git lost at least once. There's Lessie Burgess and Maggie Sutton. I'll go talk to them awhile."

Joanda saw the shoestring man standing outside the door. "Did you see a little girl with red hair take out down the sidewalk?" she asked.

The man smiled and pointed. "Way down yonder she goes like a streak o' lightnin'."

Joanda dashed through the crowd, pushing and shoving. She picked up Lolly and, spanking her soundly, brought her screaming back again.

"Found her, I see," said the shoestring man.

"Yes, sir," said Joanda. "She's all the time a-takin' off and makin' me chase after her like that. I always think she's gonna git killed, but she never does."

"Why don't you git a rope and tie her up?" asked the man.

[185]

"I jest believe I will," said Joanda, smiling.

"Don't tie me up!" screamed Lolly.

"Wants to be a grownup lady, don't she?"

"Yes, that's jest it."

Joanda realized that what the man said was true. Lolly was growing up. She was not a baby any more. She was four, and in two more years she would be starting off to school.

"I wanna play-purty," begged Lolly. "Buy me a play-purty, Nannie."

"How about shoestrings?" asked the man.

"No, she wouldn't like them . . ." Joanda had seen the shoestring man every Saturday for over two years, but had never

bought anything from him. All at once she realized he had to earn his living selling shoestrings and chewing gum.

"I'll take a pack o' gum," she said, and gave the man a nickel. She unwrapped a stick and give it to Lolly.

"Come in the store, come in the store," begged Lolly, chewing vigorously. "Buy me a play-purty like you said you would."

Ricky was leaning against the candy counter with a lollipop in his mouth. Lolly dragged her big sister from counter to counter, saying: "Buy me that! Buy me that, Nannie."

"You gonna buy her everything she asks for?" demanded Ricky.

Joanda bristled. "Nobody else buys her nothin'," she snapped. "She wants everything she sees. I all the time spend more money on her than on me."

"But you told Mama you was gonna start savin' your money. You told Uncle Shine too," said Ricky. "You jest *can't* save. Your money burns a hole in your pocket, you jest gotta . . ."

"I can too save!" retorted Joanda. "I'm jest buyin' Lolly *one* play-purty today." She looked down at her little sister. "What you want, sugar, a colorin' book?"

"Yes," said Lolly. "And colored pencils to color it with."

"All right," said Joanda firmly. She picked out a coloring book and a box of crayons and paid the clerk the money. She handed them to Lolly. "That's all you git today. See? Here's some more chewin' gum. Now let's go find Mama."

Mama and Aunt Lessie and Maggie Sutton were leaning on a counter talking about the cotton crop, just as they did every Saturday the year round. Joanda listened idly.

Cotton was their whole life. Cotton brought them joy and sorrow, hope and despair. They were part of a vast economic system too complicated to be understood, of forces too powerful to combat. But they did not know they were a part of it. They were concerned solely with the problems that faced them from day to day. Through the changing seasons of the year, they took each day as it came.

"There's only one thing to do," said Mama, "grow your cotton and git the most you can for it."

Aunt Lessie laughed. "My Pa always said—buy the wife and kids something first, give them some money to spend, and have a good time on the rest."

"Then, when the money's gone," added Maggie Sutton, "borrow some more and start all over again."

"We spend all our lives workin' off our debts," said Aunt Lessie soberly.

"And we never git 'em paid," added Mama.

"Ain't it the truth!" said Maggie Sutton.

Mama looked thoughtful. "*We're* tryin' to git out o' debt," she said. "Uncle Shine put a fool notion in our heads we'd oughta save first, and stop buyin' on the instalment plan."

"Fine!" said Aunt Lessie. "I believe in that too, but jest try to put it in practice."

"Our money gives out by Christmas," said Maggie Sutton. "Then we go hungry for two months till 'furnish' begins again in March. No matter what price we git for our cotton, I can't seem to save a penny."

Mama set her lips in a firm line. "From now on, it's gonna be different with us."

Joanda wondered. She looked up at the three women's faces and wondered if Mama were attempting the impossible. She herself knew how hard it was to keep from spending money when she had it in her pocket. Every time Lolly cried for something, no matter how badly she wanted to save, Joanda had to give in and buy it for her.

It would be hard for Mama too, because she had been used to easy spending all her life. But Joanda saw a new strength in her mother's face, and in her eyes a new dignity. The girl sensed a change—that her mother was no longer a victim of circumstance, but was making a conscious effort to control her destiny and that of her family. She was no longer going to take things just as they came. From now on she was going to *make* things be different. Filled with awe and admiration, Joanda decided to stand by her and help all she could.

Daddy came in the store with Uncle Shine, J. T. Burgess and Jed Sutton. "Let's all go to the Carnival," said the men. "Just a couple o' blocks over in the park. The kids are all out by the door waiting."

They joined the children, crossed a few lots and went into the Carnival grounds. They took rides on the merry-go-round, ferris wheel and roller-coasters. They ate ice-cream cones, popcorn and candy. Daddy and the other men shot targets at the shooting gallery, and Daddy won a large doll for Lolly and a big green blanket for Mama.

"Let's have hot tamales to eat," said Uncle Shine. "I'll treat the crowd."

The hot tamale man had moved inside the gate and was sitting on his usual chair beside his yellow cart. Uncle Shine served everybody, and in the cool evening air, the hot tamales tasted good.

Ricky took one bite of his, then gave the rest to Daddy.

"Tummy too full, son?"

"No—too hot!" cried Ricky. "Tastes like a ball o' fire. Gimme a cold drink quick!" He ran to get a Coke.

"Dave, let's go home now," said Mama.

"All right, Neva, we'll call it a day."

The Hutleys left the carnival and made their way back to the truck. They all climbed in. Lolly sat in front with Mama and Daddy; the other children stood up in back. They rode out from town on the highway, then along the dirt road between fields of cotton. The western sky was flooded with flames of red and gold, sending changing shadows across the level Arkansas landscape.

Joanda watched the setting sun as she had so many times before. She was strangely contented. For the first time she felt a deep sense of the meaning of life and of her part in it. Life would go on, bound up in cotton from year to year, changing a little but not much. Heavily-laden bolls dotted the green foliage as far as her eyes could see. She began to sing softly:

> *"Sun up in the mornin'*
> *Hot upon my back,*
> *Got to go start pickin'*
> *Cotton in my sack . . .*
>
> *Got to keep on pickin',*
> *Got to keep on pickin',*
> *Pick, pick, keep on pickin'*
> *Cotton in my sack."*

The End